IN THE SAME BOAT

'LITTLE VOICE,

RUBY SLIPPERJACK

COTEAU BOOKS
WWW.COTEAUBOOKS.COM

Editor for the Series, Barbara Sapergia.
Edited by Barbara Sapergia.
Cover painting and interior illustrations by Sherry Farrell Racette.
Cover and book design by Duncan Campbell.
"In The Same Boat" logo designed by Tania Wolk, Magpie Design.
Printed and bound in Canada by Houghton-Boston, Saskatoon.

Canadian Cataloguing in Publication Data

Slipperjack, Ruby, 1952-
Little voice

ISBN 1-55050-182-8

1. Title.
PS8587.L53L57 2001   JC813'.54   C2001-9112343
PZ7.S63194LI 2001

10 9 8 7 6 5 4 3 2 1

COTEAU BOOKS   AVAILABLE IN THE US FROM
401-2206 Dewdney Ave.   General Distrubution Services
Regina, Saskatchewan   4500 Witmer Industrial Estates
Canada S4R IH3   Niagara Falls, NY, 14305-1386

The publisher gratefully acknowledges the financial assistance of the Saskatchewan Arts Board, the Canada Council for the Arts, including the Millennium Arts Fund, the Government of Canada through the Book Publishing Industry Development Program (BPIDP), and the City of Regina Arts Commission, for its publishing program.

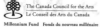

Dedicated to all grandmothers

PREFACE

JANET LUNN

"WHY AREN'T THERE ANY STORIES ABOUT US?" has been a heartfelt cry of Canadian children not descended from either French or English forebears for too long. In recent years, writers like Paul Yee, Leo Yerxa, Shizuye Takashima, and William Kurelek have created beautiful picture books and retellings of folk tales from the cultures of their ancestors. But there have been almost no children's novels, no up-to-date stories with which these children might identify.

Not more than a generation ago, this was true for all Canadian children. All but a small handful of their books came from Great Britain, France, or the United States. That is certainly not true now. Canadian children can immerse themselves happily in stories set in their own towns and countrysides, identify with characters like themselves, and be comforted and bolstered by a shared experience. This is what children of Japanese or African or indigenous North American descent have been wanting to do.

This series, *In the Same Boat,* was motivated by the desire of Coteau Books to do something about this. What a good idea it was! In these first five books for readers in their middle years of childhood, five writers, from five different backgrounds, offer the children who share these backgrounds stories in which they can recognize themselves and the way they live. At the same time, they offer all children insights into these diverse cultures.

These are five good stories, strong works of fiction, but what is perhaps more important is that they are all told honestly and with the authority that is only given to writers who truly understand what they are writing about.

LITTLE VOICE

SUMMER 1978

W E CHOKED ON THE BILLOWING DUST AS THE OLD truck bounced along the gravel road toward our house. My brother Billy and I and our little sister Cindy were sitting in the back of the truck, along with the boxes of groceries.

My name is Ray.

I looked at the boxes bouncing in front of us. Mama had bought a bag of potatoes, and onions, rice, flour, oats, baking powder, canned milk, sugar, salt, and pepper, which were packed in the three boxes in front of us. The two long boxes we were sitting on contained lard, cans of Klik, canned corned beef, a chunk of bologna, bacon, spareribs, pork hocks, and salt pork. This meat stuff was packed in inner waxed cardboard boxes. They were still cold under our butts.

This was Mama's monthly purchase of food from her welfare cheque. We always got so hungry before we could hitch our monthly ride with our neighbour, Charlie, whenever he headed to town to cash his company cheque.

Charlie used to be a good friend of our father. Dad died when a skidder overturned at the tree-cutting site about two years ago. Since then, Mama had been taking Charlie's offer to drive us into town to get groceries. That first year, people used to drop in at our house to bring food or ask how we were doing, and they would sit with Mama while we kids played outside eating the candies or whatever treats they brought. Mama had cheques coming regularly until last year. The cheques stopped coming and the people stopped coming too. Then she got welfare.

Now it was just the four of us.

These days, Mama sat alone most of the time. She just cooked our sparse meals and never said very much. We spent our time playing around our little house and going to school, but always there was the knowledge that we'd be coming home to a dark and mournful looking home. Mama hardly ever put the lights on until supper, and only for a little while before we had to go to bed. Our lunches for school were no more than bannock with a slice of Klik, most times. It was too far to walk back home for lunch from school, especially in the winter. So my brother Billy and I usually had to bring food with us to school in the morning. But I did not dwell on that too often. It was just too depressing!

I did not like school very much. In fact, I hated it! The other kids always made fun of me. They didn't bother Billy or Cindy so much. They just picked on me all the time. That was why I made sure I got all my answers correct in math and English, because I knew they would make fun of me if I got a question wrong. And I liked finding out new words and what they meant. Then I would try to figure out how to use them in a sentence. I was really good with spelling too. If only I didn't have to go to school. I wished I could do all my school work at home, but they didn't let you do stuff like that.

A big bounce over a huge pothole told me we were close to home. I watched the rocks go sailing by as they were kicked up by the tires. I pulled Cindy back by her sweater, yelling over the noise, "Don't stick your face out there, a rock will shoot up and bust your eyeball!"

Billy giggled as Cindy plopped back down beside me, her mouth still open in surprise. Her hair was cut short, just under her ears, and had bangs that touched the tops of her eyelashes. She looked cute. Billy, on the other hand, had very short hair like the rest of the men did, with longer hair at the top that kind of swung forward to his forehead in a "V" shape, and he had freckles, lots of them, that kind of looked like mud splatters that stretched from his cheeks to the top of his nose. Everyone at school called him Spots.

Finally, the truck came to a skidding stop alongside the road and we jumped down and started unloading the boxes from the back of the truck. We would still have to haul them to the top of the hill and into the stand of trees on the other side where the little, faded, run-down brown house stood. Mama said it was asking too much of Charlie to drop us right at our door, since he would have to drive all the way around to get out to the old road in front of our house.

That little old brown house was the cheapest Mama could find to rent that was still in walking distance to the school. We used to live at the company housing unit closer to the school until our father died. I never quite understood, but somehow going to school was connected to the welfare cheque that Mama got to get the food to feed us.

After we had pulled the small boxes out to the ground, Mama was there to get the big box out and then, with an irritated gesture, she slammed the truck tailgate shut. I wondered what had happened between Charlie and Mama as we hauled the boxes off the road, because we had no sooner pulled the meat box off when the truck took off in a big hurry, leaving a big swirl of dust behind it. Mama mumbled under her breath and shook her fist as the truck disappeared around the corner. I guessed that she had had another fight with Charlie. I didn't ask, and she seemed in no mood to explain to me what was happening and why Charlie was mad.

I'm the oldest of the children. And I'm a girl! It drives me crazy when boys first meet me. They have to go on and on about my name! What makes them think they have sole property to names like mine? I wouldn't have minded being Charlie or Emile, Frank or Sylvester...well, maybe not Sylvester, kind of reminds me of the cat. But, I could have been Jon or Bennet, Daniel or Henry – short for Henrietta.

What was this? Mama had just uttered a swear under her breath at Charlie. She normally never did that. From the gist of the conversation I had overheard, I guessed that perhaps he wanted to get paid for driving us to the grocery store and back. I just glanced at Mama and concentrated on getting the boxes up the hill. We got some kind of a system going where we would pile everything up on top of the hill first. Then we would get them all down the hill and into the little house one at a time.

I was ten years old now. My brother Billy was eight and Cindy was six. We lugged the first two boxes to the top of the hill. It was amazing how Billy could be there, just barely touching the box, yet make out like he was heaving and breathing, hard at work.

When we finally crowded around the kitchen area after we hauled the last box in, we surveyed the small freezer above the refrigerator for a minute, then Mama began cramming things in. She was really cramming in the pork hocks and spareribs. Half the bologna and bacon would keep for awhile in the fridge, and the other half would take up what little room there was left in the freezer.

We were all very hungry. We had just gone through another week of little more than bannock and porridge.

Finally, Mama sat sagging over the table for a full minute before she lifted her head. She looked very tired. I knew that she had just had a birthday this past week. She was twenty-eight years old. I only remembered because we had to do a family tree with birthdays one time at school. But we didn't have any special birthday parties at our house. So that was how I knew how old she actually was when I really looked at her for the first time in a long while. I suddenly felt such warmth, love, and...pity for my mama. Then, just at that moment, she brushed her long black hair off her forehead and stood up.

She had on a pair of blue jeans and a blue shirt – I think it was one of Father's shirts. She smiled at me and down at little Cindy and Billy and softly said, "Look, let's take out some of the spareribs and you know what we'll do? We'll build a little fire out back and we'll roast them over the fire, eh?" Oh, my mouth just watered at the thought!

Billy and Cindy responded in an enthusiastic chorus, "Yeah!"

And then she added, "Ray, wrap four of the potatoes with foil and we'll roast them in the fire too!" Now we all scurried about, getting ourselves cleaned up and getting things ready for supper. It was such a big deal, being able to eat such a huge meal together!

After cooking our meal over the firepit in the back yard, we laughed at Billy's jokes, and most of all, we laughed at Mama. Oh, she was so funny once she got talking about the people around here and about some old people our grandmother had told her about. I hadn't seen her in this mood in a very long time. Then she got into the stories and legends of the Ojibwa people. I suddenly had to look away, because it was at this point that my father would take up the stories. Father was not Native, but he used to tell us his own version of the English nursery rhymes.

Through blurred, teary eyes, I focussed on the flames of the fire as Mama's faltering voice became stronger. I glanced at Billy and little Cindy. They sat enraptured, as if they were hearing the stories for the first time. I glanced at Mama, but she did not look at me and continued with the stories, her eyes closed half the time. But as soon as she really got going, we were mesmerized at her descriptions and stories of a time long gone. She hinted that the things in the stories were not quite so forgotten, that if one were still attuned to such things – as Grandma had told her – they could still be there.

That was my constant childhood reminder of the ancient trickster called Weesquechak, and the Memegwesiwug who lived in the rock cliffs, and after them, nothing seemed impossible. I knew that there were those I could acknowledge without actually seeing them with my eyes, but knowing that they were very real just the same.

All too soon the mosquitoes drove us indoors, where Cindy and Billy scrambled to bed and Mama and I quietly washed the dishes and put the leftover food away. That would probably be our lunch tomorrow.

I stood by the kitchen door and I could see, between the trees, the lights from a window. The old couple who lived in that house were our closest neighbours. There were two rows of houses on the other side of the stand of trees. Ours was the last house on this gravel road, where it swung around to form a loop. The loop of the road eventually joined the main road which ran by our school. I liked not having close neighbours. We played outside and made as much noise as we wanted.

Billy liked to play Weesquechak, the trickster from one of Mama's stories. Since Weesquechak could turn himself into anything and be a man or a woman, we never knew which character Billy was until we figured out which story he was acting out.

Mama stood by the stove, hanging up the dishtowel on the oven door. The yellow linoleum on the floor was worn to the black where she stood, and there was another bald spot by the door that Mama had covered with an old woven rug she had made.

"What's the matter, Ray? You really should make an effort to smile more often. Your lovely eyes...do you remember your father's eyes? They were always filled with laughter...." Her voice trailed off as I nodded and smiled. Yes, I remembered my father's smile.

She sighed and said, "Go to bed now, and think about what you would like to do tomorrow." Tomorrow was

Sunday. Mama liked to do something with all of us on Sundays.

I turned and went down the hallway and entered the bathroom. Above the sink, a round silver-banded mirror hung by its handle. I flipped it over to the magnifying side and looked at my green eyes. They had reddish brown specks that shot out to the green. They called me Cat Eyes at school. I must have really looked odd to some people. I had dark skin and black hair like Mama, but I had green eyes like my father.

I washed my face and went into the bedroom I shared with Cindy. Billy had his own small room beside the bathroom. And Mama had her own room by herself now. Her bedroom window overlooked the hill behind the cabin where we usually played. I most often saw her standing by the window watching us. I thought she must be very lonely.

TOWARD THE END OF JULY, a taxi pulled up on the road facing our house. We did not have a driveway, as such, but more like a walking path up to the front door. The car door opened and an old woman got out of the car, very slowly. With impatient gestures, she got the driver to get her bags out of the car. When that was done, the taxi pulled away, and there stood Grandma.

Well, we descended on her like bees to honey and she gave us each a hug. We knew it wasn't often that we could expect to see Grandma, but if she did show up, all the other family members were obliged to come to that location, because she could no longer visit everyone in turn. Well, she had been at Aunt Vera's last summer and we had not been able to afford to go there, so we didn't get to see her. Then, the year when our father died, she was here with us. This year, she was supposed to be at Aunt Martha's place...so what was she doing here?

Needless to say, we didn't care. We rushed out to her, and Mama being the first there, got to the questions and soon found out that Aunt Martha's family had decided to go to Banff National Park for their holidays, and now there was Grandma in front of us! Mama, Billy, and Cindy all shouted and hooted for joy. I mean, if you get one visitor a year, and it happens to be your grandma, it makes it that much more precious! I just stood there as a very warm feeling slowly came over me.

I remembered the first time I ever saw Grandma. We had gone to visit her at her cabin in a small community along the railroad tracks. Mama told me once that it took about two hours on the train to get there. I was very small then. Grandma had a wheelbarrow in front of her cabin, and I would ride around in it all day with her pushing me. She'd wheel me down the path to the lake and up to the cabin again. I especially remembered her laughter.

The last time I'd seen her was the image that had stayed with me in the past two years. It was about a week after my father's funeral and she was going home. We had been at the train station and she had stood with her arms around Mama, rocking her back and forth. Now she was back again.

So that week we had the mother of our own mother in the house, and Billy and Cindy always wanted attention. I had only one burning question to ask and the time just never seemed right. I wanted to know if I could go and live with Grandma over the winter months and go to school there, since it was getting almost unbearable for me to go to school here. The constant harassment from the other kids had really got me feeling angry and helpless all the time. Mama had told me never to talk back to them, so now I didn't talk to anyone at all!

I knew that there were many discussions between Mama and Grandma about that, but it became evident that Mama could not afford the one child less on her child welfare payment. And so began my one-girl suffering for the sake of our family's income.

Grandma's visit was short because my other aunt could not come to visit us. We went blueberry picking with Grandma, whatever little berries were left, that is. But we did not care. She walked slowly and talked slowly. Our Ojibwa language wasn't all that good, so we listened, but Cindy and Billy's responses always came out in English. She'd grudgingly answer them in her broken English. Slowly, she would wind her way around the bushes, carefully picking only the bigger berries out of each berry patch.

"Leave some for the bears," she would say. It was their

food, after all. And so, we did. We knew what it meant to be hungry, and the poor bear coming to eat and finding out that we had picked everything would not be very nice indeed.

I found I only counted the days before Grandma would have to leave, not the days she had left to be with us. And so, when it was time for her to get to the train station, I had counted to day "o" and there was nothing else to look forward to. She came out to me then, at the time when she had arranged for the taxi to pick her up. I sat by the tree beyond the fire, where I always sat while I waited for the things that had to happen to finish happening. Like when the people came after Father's funeral...I had decided that place was the best place to sit.

I heard Grandma's slow steps coming up behind me. I wondered why she was taking the time to see me. Her taxi would be coming soon. I had already said goodbye to her in my mind; now she was intruding in my silent space. What did she want? I looked up at her and smiled. I waited. She, in her usual slow way, settled down on the rock beside me and sat for a full minute before she glanced at me and spoke.

"Your mama says you are still not saying very much. Last year, you hardly said anything at all. The year before, when your father died, you had stopped speaking altogether. I have seen your spurts of happiness and enthusiasm. We have been happy together. We have even laughed together...but you do not speak, Naens."

She sighed and continued. "Naens – 'Little Voice.' That was not what your name was supposed to mean, was it?" I shook my head, no. Grandma always called me "Naens," because there was no "R" in the Ojibwa language, so an "N" was used instead. So Ray became "Nay," and "Little Ray" became "Naens," and "naens" actually does mean "little voice" in Ojibwa. Therefore, my name became Little Voice.

She leaned over closer to me and her black eyes bore into mine, as she said with great authority, "Naens, you must now come forward with your voice or someone else will take it away from you who is not supposed to have it!"

That alarmed me. "What do you mean?" I asked.

She smiled and whispered, "You know very well that if we have the knowledge and the skill to do something and do not do it, there will be someone else that will do it...don't you? They will take and run off with the knowledge of Naens, because she could not speak to say it was hers."

That was the end of that weird conversation. We heard the honk of the taxi and I gave her a light hug and she took her slow, unhurried time back up the walkway to the house.

I was very sad and depressed most of the month of August and, when September came around, I had absolutely no wish to go back to school, but that was the only way we would get something to eat. I started hanging around at the hairdresser's shop to pass the time on the weekends. Delores, the lady that owned the shop, was very nice, and sometimes she would let me sit and watch her do the ladies' hair. She was funny.

Across the street from Delores's place was the gas station, and beside it was the only Chinese restaurant in town. There was actually only one street running along the length of the town, with businesses on both sides. On one side was the movie theatre, a big parking lot, a shoe shop, the grocery store where we got our groceries, and its own large parking lot beside it. Then there was the bank and a large government building. Across the street was the hardware store, a lumberyard, the other restaurant, a parking lot, and the post office at the far end of the street close to the train station. The building beside the hairdresser's shop was the laundromat.

The people were nice, the adults at least. Nobody paid much attention to me. Most of the guys worked for the forest and lumber company or for the railway and the government offices. Everybody else worked in the businesses and shops. Up the hill, away from the business end, stood the two churches, one on each side of a huge clump of trees.

The only high school stood between the churches and there was another elementary school further away toward the end of town. Our school, the one closer to our house, was between Delores's shop and the railway tracks. That was where the businessmen's and government workers' kids went to school. That was also why the kids always made sure I knew that I didn't belong there. There weren't many Native children going to that school.

I did not take to the first week of school very well. As the months went by, I became very angry and resentful at the chants and poems the other kids would direct at me when they noticed that I wore the same dress twice in one week! They made fun of my shoes, which were all right for my jeans but not for the dresses I had to wear to school. I said not a thing and kept bottling everything inside me. Every time something happened, I would imagine which shelf I would put it on. Each of my shelves, which existed only in my mind, had titles ranging from Stupid Thing to Ignorant Thing, Dumb Thing, Nothing, and Idiot.

As soon as this thought entered my mind, there came the picture of Jamie, the red-haired boy sitting beside me in Grade Six. After a history class about Native people one day, he stopped as he was going out in front me, held the door open for me to go by, and said, "Indians first!" I stared at him and he glanced away as I slipped by. What was the use! I couldn't think of a thing to say to him. I wasn't ever going to bother to talk to anybody again! I filed that under "Idiot."

When I got to the road to home that afternoon after school, I kicked at the packed snow pile so hard that I cracked the stitching on the side of my boot. Now, I knew very well that the hole would just get bigger and begin to eat the snow and drink water, mud, and everything else it brushed against, until it had such a huge mouth that my whole foot would just slide right out! I noticed that not only had my mind grown tired of filling up the shelves in my brain with all kinds of junk, but it had also gained a sense of humour somewhere along the way.

Like, the other day our science teacher was holding a frog up for us to see. You know the kind? The frogs they keep in the huge bottles full of stinky water? Well, he stood up there in front of the class and said, "I would like one of you to tell me what this is."

I happened to be in front of him at the time and my mind as always responded with a rather loud voice saying, "Why, sir! It looks exactly like you! Son of yours, maybe?" I turned to the window and let my smile disappear before I dared to turn around.

That was when he looked directly at me and said, "You! What is this?"

I answered, just barely above a whisper. "My name is Ray."

He cleared his throat and asked me, "Well then, Ray. What is this?"

I glanced down at the floor. What kind of an idiotic question was that? We all knew that it was a frog. Maybe he was asking what kind of frog it was. I shrugged. I didn't know what those kind of frogs were called in English.

That was when one of the boys at the back of the class

shouted, "It's a frog, sir!" Suddenly there was a rush of air that exploded from my chest as I caught my breath on a laugh, but it was too late! The snots in my nose gushed out the same time as I clamped my hand over my mouth. I was now so embarrassed, I instantly lost my urge to laugh. Now what could I do? The teacher had gone on talking about the frog. I quickly got out of my seat and hurried out the door to the bathroom across the hall. After washing my face as quickly as I could, I went back to the classroom.

Then there was the afternoon outside the school when the class decided to go throw around some large jam cans filled with ice, with crude wooden handles frozen at the top. I had never seen anything so stupid in all my life! We were supposed to push these jam cans across a frozen water path toward some red and blue markings at the other end. I was not impressed. After a whole afternoon of this, I still did not get the point!

On the way home that day, we met Hitz. I think his name came from the habit he had of a half-cough before he began to speak, so that his sentences always began with "H'it's." Anyway, there was Hitz coming toward us on our way home. Cindy and Billy ran on by him, but he stopped in front of me and said, "H'it's going to be another cold day tomorrow, I see."

He rocked in his rubber boots, looking up at the sky. His fur trapper's cap slipped to the back of his bushy grey-haired head as he looked up at the sky. He had on at least several coats that I could see, the top red-checkered one being very stiff with dirt and threadbare, with holes in the sleeves. His pants were also very dirty and there looked to be about three inches of gathered cuffs above his protruding rubber boots.

He was always at the store when we went for groceries, but he never spoke to Mama. He did tell me once, though, that he knew our grandfather, my father's dad, and that they had been very good friends. I remember my father saying once that his dad was the only one who came to visit after he married Mama. His other family members decided we did not exist. I couldn't remember this. Father's dad had died when I was about three years old.

I liked Hitz. He always gave us a candy, after nodding to Mama for her okay. Now, here he was in front of me. I too looked up at the sky but didn't say anything. Then he did a side-step shuffle to position himself out of my way.

"You are Ray. Do you know why they call you Ray?" he asked.

I shook my head. I had never thought about it. He looked up at the sky again and shoved his hands into his pant pockets.

"Well," he said, "you were born at the first ray of sunlight in the early morning...July, wasn't it?" July 16th, I thought to myself, but didn't say anything. "Your grandpa Raymond gave you that name."

Somehow, that pleased me very much. Why hadn't Mama ever told me that? I smiled up at him, and then he took a big giant step away from me and I ran to catch up with Cindy and Billy.

After that, I always stopped to talk to Hitz whenever I saw him. He was a nice old man. He lived in an old decrepit shack right at the edge of town. The very last cabin. Charlie told us all about him one time when he had to stop there to pick up Hitz before he drove us all to the grocery store. But lately, Charlie did not bother to pick up Hitz. That was why Hitz was now walking into town.

When we got home, I threw off my coat and asked Mama, "Why was I called Ray?" She glanced at me, but she was busy with Cindy at the door, getting wet socks off and telling Billy to take off his boots before he went into the kitchen. I waited patiently as I went about setting the kitchen table as usual.

Finally, when she came back into the kitchen, she said, "Well, now, let me see. That was a very long time ago. I would have to say it was your grandfather who gave you that name. As I remember, he was all hell-bent on seeing his first grandson that he was going to name Raymond, after himself. So when you showed up, he said he'd call you Ray anyway...said something about the sun coming up just then. Sun Ray, or something of the sort. Anyway, Ray you became and Ray you are now.... Take the macaroni off the stove before it boils over!"

I grabbed the pot, thinking that it would have been nice to have known Grandpa Raymond. That name had a very nice sound to it. I drained the macaroni, set it on the table, and went to put my notebooks away. I had homework to do again tonight.

LIFE IN TOWN

THE SNOW CAME DOWN AND DOWN, AND CONTINUED TO come down as the days stretched into December. I now refused altogether to talk in school. Most times I just sat by the window and watched the snow come down. I wondered what Grandma was doing. What was it like where she was? Was there someone to get wood for her, to get her groceries? I knew that there was no running water where she was. That meant she would have to go to the lake and chip a hole in the ice to get the water for her cabin. I would gladly do that for her. That would be fun. I wanted to go live with her so badly, I would take a big breath of the cold, crisp, morning air and imagine that she was taking the same breath of air just at that very moment.

On early cold mornings, our boots crunched against the frozen snow as we trudged down the street, to the right and up the hill to where the school stood. As we approached, Billy would run up to his classmates by the sidewalk, Cindy would run to the playground, and I...I just walked up the sidewalk, slowly pushing the door open and heading to my locker. I would throw my jacket, boots, and lunch into the locker, put on my running shoes, grab my books, and slam the door shut and snap the lock. Then I would slowly wander to the home-room and sit down.

There I would sit, looking out the window, and totally ignore the students who came in one after the other, and at the end of the long procession, the teacher would enter. He had a way of slamming his books on the desk and exclaiming that it was the...whatever date it was. Like we didn't even know what day it was. While I, on the other hand, had begun a countdown the minute school started. I was only interested in how many more days we had to spend in this class!

November had come and gone. I had suffered through Thanksgiving and Halloween. Mama didn't have enough money for extra food treats, so we had partridge stew and dumplings. Oh, that was the best meal we ever had! Hitz had given me the bag with four partridges when I met him on the road that Friday afternoon after school.

Mama was actually very happy and excited that we got to eat something from the wild.

She was always craving for fish, but the lake was a bit too far away to walk to and, besides, we didn't have a boat or canoe. Mama and Dad used to walk down the railroad tracks to set some rabbit snares in the winter when they could see the rabbit tracks, but she didn't do that any more.

I thought maybe she would go if I offered to come with her. But who would look after Billy and Cindy? Maybe if we had a toboggan, we could pull Cindy in that...but we would have to buy a toboggan.

That was when I decided to try to earn some money and buy some things like that with it. Maybe I could even save enough money to go see Grandma! Yes, that was what I would do. I worked anyway I could and saved all my money! That was the beginning of my walk through the streets after school and on weekends, asking if anyone wanted their driveways shovelled. In the summer, I could water their gardens or something. And then I discovered babysitting.

At the grocery store, I introduced myself to mothers with children and told them where I lived if they ever wanted a babysitter. Mama wasn't sure she liked that idea at first, but after she met either one of the parents when they came to get me to babysit, she didn't say anything about it again.

One afternoon, we had decided to meet Mama at the grocery store instead of coming straight home as we usually did. Billy, Cindy, and I arrived at the grocery store and immediately spotted Charlie's truck outside. Billy and Cindy ran inside, all excited, and I was ready to rush inside also, when I noticed Hitz. He was hovering around, just outside the area of the store. I immediately felt that there was something very wrong. So, while the others ran inside the store, I turned and walked toward Hitz. As usual, I did not say anything, but stopped within the vicinity where I would feel his body's presence, where there would be no need to talk.

After a few minutes, he came closer and I remained still, trying to understand what he was feeling. Then he gave a big deep intake of air and I looked up. I saw great big tears rolling down his wrinkled old begrizzled cheeks and disappearing down the folds of his jowls and throat. I didn't move. I ducked my head down to see that his hands hung limp at his sides. I knew this poor old man had just received the worst blow of his life and that there was absolutely no one around...or maybe no one around who cared.

Suddenly, both his hands shot out and held both of mine. In that moment, I felt his pain. I felt his anguish. I looked up, and as I watched his silent teardrops start rolling down his cheeks, I suddenly felt my own warm tears flood my eyes. This surprised me very much, because I hadn't been able to cry when I'd heard my father died. I hadn't been able to cry when I saw his dead body, and I hadn't been able to cry when they buried him. Now here was Hitz in front of me and...we started bawling together. I started crying so hard, he grabbed me and held me tight, and I cried harder as I felt my anguish and his sorrow wash through me. Finally, as if remembering where we were, he pulled me to the side of the building.

"I am so sorry, my Sun Ray. I did not mean to upset you, but you see...I have just found out...just now, when they took me to the police station...my only brother...my baby brother was killed in a car accident in Toronto.... Oh, he's gone! He's gone...and I never even saw him grown up! Oh, he was just a little handsome lad when I saw him last...but, oh, how I loved him so! Oh, how I loved him so!"

I threw my arms around him and just held him tight. It was all I could do. It was some moments before I felt his arms come around me. Then we just stood still for what seemed like a good five minutes before Mama showed up at the grocery store door yelling, "Ray! Ray! Where are you?"

I gave Hitz a peck of a kiss on the cheek, then turned and ran into the store. When she saw me, Mama grabbed me and whispered in my ear, "You have been crying, Ray?"

I nodded and hugged her. "Hitz was crying. His little brother is dead."

Her arms came around me and she held me still several minutes before she said, "Yes, we heard about it. Ray, his little brother was seventy-two years old." She let me go, and by then, it was time to load the boxes on Charlie's truck. I thought about the many old men I had seen in town without realizing that they would be someone's "baby brother." I felt a smile touch my face as Charlie's truck attacked the gravel road with a vengeance.

The next thing after this was the Christmas pageant. I hated the idea the moment our enthusiastic teacher announced it. Oh, I did not want to be on stage! I could not be on stage! I was absolutely and totally against being on stage! So when the day came that he announced what the show was going to be about and who was going to play what part, I volunteered to be the straw in the manger before anyone got to say anything! Well, that got everyone into such merry laughter that it gave me time to figure out what else I could be and I announced that I was going to be the star, before anyone else got the chance.

And so I was the star in the nativity scene of the play. I made a huge star covered in foil from a popcorn foil box, and there I was on the night of the play, standing around like an idiot until my time came. I knew Mama was not going to be in the audience, because she had to take care of Billy and Cindy, but I knew Hitz and Charlie would be there, because Charlie's Jonathan was one of the sheep.

I came in on cue, but just as I entered the stage, there was a big commotion. It took me a bit to figure out that the cardboard box manger was on fire! A candle from one of the disciples had set the straw around the manger on fire! People were scurrying about to put the fire out, but then the baby blanket in the manger caught fire and then the baby Jesus was on fire! Mary and Joseph were scrambling about, trying to save the baby Jesus, when one of the wise men's paper coats caught on fire and then the cardboard sheep started crumbling into the flames.... Well, the next thing you knew, the whole place was full of smoke and there I was standing with my Star of Bethlehem amidst the smoke and commotion! The water sprinklers came on just then, and men ran about stomping on the straw and the baby Jesus and the sheep.

Suddenly, Hitz materialized at the edge of the stage and

he was laughing his head off! All I could see was the gaping hole of his mouth. I too began to laugh and, between the two of us, I didn't hear anything else! I scrambled off stage and fell into his arms as we stood back and laughed at the confusion. That was best pageant ever!

We made our way to the front of the auditorium, where Charlie suddenly stuck his hand under my arm and declared, "Come, I'd best take you home."

Hitz disappeared and I followed Charlie and Jonathan out the door to their truck. I said nothing at all until they dropped me off at the bottom of the hill. Then I said, "Thanks, Charlie, and I'll see you at school tomorrow, Jonathan."

They did not immediately drive off, and I heard Jonathan say, "She's weird, Dad. I mean, she never says anything to anybody except that old man Hitz. And when she does, she says that 'polite proper stuff' like she's better than we are! I hate her!"

I stood quite still. I didn't think I was stuffy or phoney! What was he talking about? I didn't remember a time when he had bothered to stop and say anything to me! So I reasoned that if a person had not bothered to talk to you before, they had no reason to say bad things about you! Well, then, I hated him too! I trudged up the hill, and as soon as I came over the top, I saw our cabin with smoke coming up the chimney. That was home. That was where Mama and Billy and Cindy were. I ran down the hill toward the back door.

We were intent on having decorations for our little cabin, but as Mama had explained to us so many times before, we couldn't afford to buy any. But on one of my babysitting jobs, I came across decorations that Delores, the hairdresser, used. They were made of cigarette foil and she rolled them on pencils, scrunched them down and pulled the pencil out, and rolled them into a circle, and they became little foil circles! Many of those were strung around a string and they looked very beautiful. These were criss-crossed by shiny candy foil folders of red, blue, and green, and by silver ribbons that complemented the silver cigarette foils.

I got my brother and little sister to collect the foils from the cigarette bins and candy store bins. We had collected quite a few before we got to work one weekend at our kitchen table.

Mama watched us for quite awhile and then decided that this year we would go and cut a real Christmas tree! We were all excited as we set out with an axe. Down the railroad tracks we went, one mile and then another mile, before we spotted a tree that would fit our little living room area just right. We went down into the ditch and scampered up the hill to the site. That was when Mama noticed the rabbit tracks.

"I bet I could set a snare here before Christmas and maybe we would have a roast rabbit for the Christmas meal!" she exclaimed.

I smiled. I hadn't seen her so excited about anything in

a long time. So we went home with the tree and, while Billy and Cindy decorated the tree, Mama and I went back with the snare wire. She set the snares right along the rabbit path. We went home smiling and talking about what a big feast we would have at Christmas!

When we pushed the door open, there stood the tree with all the glitter we had gathered! I was so proud of Billy and Cindy – they had sure done a great job. And Mama made a special treat for us. She melted sugar in a pot and then she went outside and poured the melted sugar into the snow by the porch in many swirls, which immediately crystalized into sugar swirls! We went to bed, very happy and full of excitement for the next day.

That morning, it seemed as if it was the first time I had looked around our home. The back door had a little porch where we piled the garbage and tubs. There were three bedrooms and a bathroom. The kitchen was by the front door and opened out into a larger room where the kitchen table and couch stood. There were gold drapes at the big window and there was a window by the stove. The light was on in the kitchen and I could tell that Mama was making coffee, because I smelled it immediately when I entered the room.

For the first time in a long while, I felt a lift of happiness as I walked across the room to the kitchen. Suddenly, I stopped dead still. I had not realized I was smiling until I felt my face fall and the painful ache in my heart dropped back into place full force! I saw Mama standing by the counter, looking out the window beside the coffee pot, and

I saw her shoulders shake. I knew she was crying. Oh, Mama! I did not know if I should go quietly back to my room or go into the kitchen and hug her to me. I knew she still had quiet crying bouts for Father, but I knew she never wanted us to know.

I decided to start straightening things out by the back door. I found the mitts Cindy had lost and Billy's old thick socks that he'd set up a big stink about last week. I piled the things up that needed washing and put the spring rubber boots into a separate section beside the trash bin. When I was done, I entered the kitchen, and there was Mama sitting at the table with a cup of coffee, smiling at me.

"Well, Ray. What shall we do today?"

Today was Saturday. We'd had the last day of school yesterday. Christmas was on Wednesday, so we had a good...what? Four days to get ready for Christmas! I smiled and pulled up a chair by the table. She filled a cup of coffee and pushed it across the table to me. I relished the feel of being a "grown up" with a cup of coffee. I piled in the sugar and milk until it barely had a tinge of brown to it. Mama smiled and giggled at me.

It was then that a thought popped into my head. I had ten dollars saved from my babysitting money and odd jobs I had been doing. I was always trying to save money to buy a ticket to Grandma, but I realized now that the best thing I could give Mama would be a RADIO! She would love to have a radio to keep her company while we were in school. I couldn't wait until the store opened! In the meantime, I would have to try to keep my excitement down and concentrate on what special things we could give the kids.

Mama smiled and said, "I saved five dollars from the last bill I had to pay for groceries. How should we spend it?"

I said, "Why don't we take Cindy and Billy to the show and leave them there. Come back here and check our snares and hide some candies. I bought a bag of candies when I babysat for Dorothy the last time. So, we could bag them into little Christmas presents."

Mama laughed. "Oh, Ray! You're always way ahead of me! I also had a few dollars set aside for candies, so now what do we do with my money?"

I smiled at her. "We have lard and flour and I know you can make a really delicious pie. We didn't have a freezer for the blueberries we picked this year, but I saw some frozen blueberries at the store."

She laughed aloud and leaned back in her chair. "Oh, Ray. You are wonderful! I will buy some fresh-frozen blueberries, because I really do hate the canned stuff. We'll make blueberry pies and roasted rabbits for Christmas."

I beamed at her, but her eyes suddenly filled with tears again. I looked away and pretended I was stirring my coffee, and then she said, "Oh, my Ray, I do love you so! I don't think I've told you that in such a long time."

She sipped her coffee and I looked up at her. "You know when Hitz was crying? I wasn't thinking about Hitz at all. I felt bad about that...you see, I was thinking about Dad. I always wished I could have cried then. I felt like I was bad because I couldn't show him how sad I was when he died...but I just couldn't. Then, when I saw Hitz cry, I hoped Dad knew I was crying for him. Do you think he knows that? I really want him to know I miss him and...that I loved him so much."

Now it was my turn, stirring my coffee and glancing out the window, trying to distract myself so I didn't completely burst into tears.

When I glanced at Mama, she had put her feet up on the chair beside me. "Ray," she said, "your father knows how much you love him. He also knows how much I love him and so do Billy and Cindy. Just because he's not here at the moment, doesn't mean he's not around. Sometimes I feel his presence so near, I feel I could almost touch him."

Just then, Billy and Cindy came bursting into the room. What was it that smelled so good? I had been so intent on the discussion, I hadn't noticed the delicious smell coming out of the oven! Mama jumped up. "Oh, my! I totally forgot about the cinnamon buns! Thank you for the talk, Ray." I smiled as she hurried to take the delicious-smelling buns out of the oven and set them down on the table.

The sun was now throwing shadows from the surrounding trees right across our front yard. The sunrise had been absolutely pink and orange. It was going to be a wonderful day! From a corner hidden in the cupboard, Mama pulled out a box of hot chocolate, and this she mixed with canned milk and water and it was absolutely wonderful! We laughed, talked, and told stories of all our "adventures," as we called them, on any given day.

On the whole, our Christmas that winter was just wonderful. Mama actually caught two rabbits from her snares and we met Hitz again the next day and he gave us four more. So we had roasted rabbits, fried rabbits, and stewed rabbits with dumplings.

Billy and Cindy helped me wrap the radio I had bought for Mama. It was black on the front and wood all around, with shiny silver knobs on the front. It looked very nice! On Christmas morning, we all brought it to the kitchen table and set it down in front of Mama.

We had coloured the brown paper wrapping with flowers and leaves to make it pretty. She looked at us and very slowly she unwrapped the paper. When she saw the radio, she burst into tears! Billy and Cindy stared at me with eyes wide open. Then Mama started laughing and said it was the best present she had ever received! Oh, that was a wonderful Christmas!

Every morning since then, the first thing I heard when I woke up was the sound of music from the radio and the smell of coffee coming from the kitchen.

I never saw Hitz though, during the Christmas week. I heard later that he had gone to visit his family in southern Ontario somewhere.

FIRST SUMMER WITH GRANDMA

SUMMER 1979

THE DAY FINALLY CAME WHEN WE SAT WAITING AT THE train station. I was on my way to see Grandma! Billy and Cindy were running around the station playing hide-and-seek, and Mama sat beside me on the bench that leaned against the station wall.

"I wish I was coming with you," she said. I smiled, looking at the kids as they ran by us again. "But I will enjoy the peace and quiet, I think." Mama laughed and grabbed Cindy as she came dashing by again. Just then, the train came around the bend. My heart was pounding with excitement as, after giving everyone hugs and kisses, I climbed aboard the train.

The train coach smelled of smoke as I walked down the aisle and found a vacant seat where I could see Mama and the kids. With a sudden clanging lurch, the train began to move. I waved to Mama and they all waved back. The train went faster and faster. I sat and waited for the conductor to come and take my ticket.

The train stopped at several towns on the way and more people got on. Sometimes I saw houses go by, but mostly the land was all lakes, trees, rocks, and more trees. After awhile, I noticed my neck was getting sore from looking out the window for so long. Then the conductor came and pulled my destination slip off my window saying, "Next stop."

My heart began pounding again as I got ready to get off. The train slowed down, but all I saw was a sandpit and several houses in behind some trees. I turned my head and realized that the station was on the other side! A lot of people stood around watching the train as I made my way to the door.

I held on to my suitcase tightly as I carefully stepped off the train, and then Grandma was there! She guided me through the crowd as the people smiled and made way for her to pass. The train began to move again as we walked beside it.

When the train finally went by, we were able to talk, and I glanced back to see that all the people were gone. "What were they all doing, Grandma?"

Grandma laughed and said, "Oh, they just came to see who was getting off and who was getting on the train." We walked along the railway tracks, and I saw the back of the train disappear around the bend far ahead of us.

Grandma's soft shoes made no noise on the black-tarred ties. Her dress was well over her knees, and all I could see were her brown stockings with white socks pulled up over her ankles. She wore a blue sweater, buttoned only at the top, and her black tam was on her head. Her braids hung on each side of her chest. She said, "Better keep an eye where you're stepping, or you'll end up kissing the ties." I giggled and concentrated on matching her step.

I didn't see the path until Grandma stepped off the tracks and headed toward a small opening in the thick bushes. The air was cooler in the shade as I followed Grandma's heels down the narrow path. Soon, we came out of the bush and there was the back of her cabin.

I saw the trees beyond the field in front of her cabin. I knew that was where the lake was! I remembered this place. I ran around to the front of the cabin, checked out the outhouse, and ran back to the cabin again. Grandma was already inside and my suitcase was on top of a bunk in the corner of the room.

She was just as excited as I was, because I noticed that there were two boxes all packed and two packsacks ready to go. She had already packed up and we were going camping! All I had time to do was to change my clothes, and then I began running back and forth with the stuff to the lake while Grandma packed the canoe.

NOW HERE WE WERE, me at the front of the canoe swinging my paddle back and forth. I was finally getting the hang of it. I had never been in a canoe before in my whole life! I paused often to look at the shimmering water and the little crests of waves that splashed against the canoe. Several seagulls came to check us out, and I was sure that one of them kept circling by just to get another cackling laugh at me. I turned to glance back at Grandma. "He's laughing at me, isn't he?"

We paddled past Mile One portage and were heading to Grandma's regular campsite beside the railroad at Mile Two portage. Suddenly, I became aware that she was not paddling anymore. I paused too and waited. She said, "Why don't we go across the portage here and check out the other big lake yonder? We would have to cross this portage, go across the railroad tracks, cross another portage, and then we would be at the lake with the river."

I turned and grinned back at her. Grandma and I decided to portage right out of the area and go into the other lake. After taking our time crossing the Mile One portage, we paddled along a long skinny lake until we came to another portage. We could still see the railroad tracks at this point, but this portage was very muddy and just teeming with mosquitoes! Large mosquitoes!

I scampered over the portage as quickly as I could, gathering as many of our things as possible, so that Grandma didn't have to go back at all. She walked slowly and I didn't want to waste any more time than was necessary. So, while she unloaded the canoe, I ran through the portage and deposited a load on the other side, then loaded up again for the last few things while she got the canoe ready. When I came back, I took the front of the canoe and she carried the back end. Thus we crossed the portage. The little canoe wasn't all that heavy, we just had to walk very slowly because Grandma was very careful not to trip or twist an ankle. When we finally set the canoe down on the other side, she had a huge beaming smile. Yeah, we did it! I giggled. I loved her very much, just then.

When we entered the other lake, it led into another narrow channel. As we paddled, it gradually widened, and soon we went past a tall rock cliff. Grandma trailed her paddle as she rummaged around in her packsack. I glanced back as she pulled out a pouch. "Tobacco," she said. "This is my tobacco pouch. At every rock cliff we come across, I will put a pinch of tobacco for the Memegwesiwug, the Rock People."

"I remember the story about the Memegwesi girl who married a Native man," I said. She gave me a big smile. She seemed very pleased that I remembered who the Memegwesiwug were. I let the canoe drift until I felt her weight shift as she reached to deposit a pinch of tobacco on a rock shelf. She said, "The one thing they don't have is tobacco, and they sure appreciate the offering when they get it. In return, they will find ways to thank us."

The canoe drifted free, and as we paddled on again I heard her say, "Remember that story about the hunter who found a hurt Memegwesi and he helped him? When the hunter left to go home, the two fish he carried in his sack got heavier and heavier, until he could hardly carry the load by the time he got home. When he dumped out his sack, it was full of big fat fish!" I smiled, remembering the time she told us that story. I also knew that the Memegwesi can paddle right toward a rock wall and disappear through it.

When we came around a point, I could see a sand beach where the sound of the river was coming from. She steered the canoe to the shoreline to the west where there was a level sloping rock to the shore, bordered with a stand of cedar trees. It was nearing evening when we got there. I could tell that this was a campsite. The tent poles were leaning against a tree.

She pulled the canoe up in a shady little bay beside the campsite and turned it over amongst the thick stand of small cedars. You could not see the canoe from the lake unless you practically stood over it. We set up the tent and got our evening meal cooked. She made bannock over the fire and cooked the other half of the pickerel we'd had at lunch time.

We ate our supper rather quickly, because Grandma had decided she wanted to set some rabbit snares behind us in the thick woods while I covered the tent floor with pine branches. I worked quickly and silently. I had just finished piling up five clumps of branches when a loon decided to come and investigate the activity. I sat on a rock by the shore and watched him. He came really close and began his bath. He had one foot sticking way out, while his beak was scratching and washing under it and his other foot kept paddling. As a result, he kept going around and around in circles. I giggled. He looked ridiculous! Then he turned and looked at me. That was when I noticed his eyes were red. I'd never known loons had red eyes!

I could hear Grandma's axe by the bay. I decided to hurry and put the branches down. I started at the entrance as Grandma had showed me, and marched the branches towards the back of the tent, like feathers all in a row, and then placed the next row slightly behind the first row and so on. I gradually worked my way right to the back of the tent. Oh, I was so proud of myself! The floor looked really good! I hated to cover up my work, but I had to spread the blankets out.

We spent about four days there, all by ourselves. We went blueberry picking along the shoreline, set rabbit snares, and had roasted rabbit for supper each evening. We also had fried fish during lunch that we caught in our fishnet. We had a wonderful time and I was very happy. Then, one evening, two canoes arrived. Two families crammed in the two canoes. They noticed our campfire and decided to set up camp beside us at the sand beach to our right. I resented the intrusion but didn't say anything. Grandma went to investigate and visit, and I didn't see her again until I had gone to bed. She came in late and said that I should have come when she did not return. She'd had a good meal of moose meat that they had cooked. I didn't answer. I was not interested in moose meat! I just hoped they would be gone by morning!

The next day, two women came to visit, along with their two young boys. I left. I went along the shoreline and picked berries and tried to find rabbit trails. I wasn't interested in visiting or seeing those people. When I returned in the afternoon, it was to find Grandma gone. I knew she'd gone visiting again, because the canoe was still there. I felt abandoned. As soon as they showed up, she disappeared!

I went into the tent and lay down. I had been there for several hours when I began to get hungry. I wondered if she'd even gone to check her rabbit snares. I got up and flipped open the birchbark basket in the corner by the front door. There were two rabbits already cleaned. I decided I would roast them over the fire as I had seen her do many times. She would be happy to find her supper already cooked when she returned. I smiled at the thought. She would be very happy with me. She would be very proud.

Very carefully, I banked up the ashes, good and hot, and propped the rabbits over the coals. I was just deciding what to do about bannock, whether I should try another batch or not because my first one had been a disaster, when Grandma came up the path from the sand beach. "Oh, I was just coming to get you. We didn't have to cook our meal tonight. They have already fed me and I was just coming to get you to come and eat over there."

I glanced up. "I don't want to go there. I will eat here. Is it all right that I started to cook the rabbits?"

She stopped for a second and looked down at me, then she sat down beside me. "There is a very pregnant woman with them. She is the sister of one of the women who came here...." I did not respond, but watched the juice start to sizzle off the rabbits. She continued. "She has another month to go, but she is having problems. They know that I am a midwife, and so they have decided to hang around until they know for sure that she will be all right."

I glanced up and asked, "Where is her husband? Isn't he supposed to look after her?" My voice came out harsh and resentful.

She glanced at me sharply, and it was a full minute before she answered me in a calm voice. "She has just come back from the hospital, where they told her every-thing was fine. They are on their way to the woman's hus-band, who is at their cabin at the trapline, about five lakes up. The two families plan to stay with the woman and her husband until they have to fly her out of there to the hos-pital, and then they'll wait for her to come back and stay with them to help with the baby until springtime. But until then...well, here they are."

I said nothing else, but my resentment was still thick, edging on anger at their unwelcome intrusion. I bit my tongue and said nothing. They came for her sometime during the afternoon. Grandma, the midwife, went to deliver a baby.

Now it was close to evening, so I got up from lying around on my blanket and made myself a bannock, jam, and butter sandwich. I wandered along the shoreline, away from the campsite, picking blueberries as I went until I filled my little jam can.

When I returned, there was still no one around and it was very hot. It was July 16th or 17th, I didn't know which, but I was eleven years old now. I could hear squirrels chattering away in the bush, but other than that, it was very quiet. After I put the little can down on the rock table beside the tent, I stood around for a bit, then decided to go down to the lake. I wandered around by the shore again, until I got to the little bay and looked at Grandma's canoe turned over on the cedar patch.

I decided I would paddle it out to the lake where I could cool off a bit from the oppressive heat. I turned the canoe over carefully and pulled it into the water. I picked up one paddle and left the other one there, and I gingerly got into the canoe and paddled...left and then right to keep it going straight. I knew that was not how it was supposed to be paddled, but I didn't know how to make it go straight by paddling only from one side the way Grandma did. Well, I managed to get out along the weeds by the bay, and decided I would play hide-and-seek and see if I could sneak away from the campsite without being seen. Much like a captive escaping from the enemy camp!

I paddled slowly, and the canoe glided over the weeds until I got past the little island by the shore and was satisfied no one had seen me. Then I paddled to the middle of the lake, but by then I was sweating hot. It was about that point that a gentle wind finally started. It was such a relief to feel some breeze. I put the paddle inside the canoe and edged myself down until I was lying flat. I could hear little waves lapping at the sides of the canoe. I closed my eyes and let myself drift out into the open water.

I must have fallen asleep, for the next thing I knew, I heard rushing water! Where was that coming from? I sat up and saw that I was very close to the rapids of the river and it was almost dark! I grabbed the paddle and tried to turn the canoe, but it took off right toward the rapids instead! I switched to the other side and paddled hard, but suddenly the canoe whipped about and it was once again being pulled hard toward the huge, white, foaming water! The current grabbed the canoe and hurled it against a rock that whipped it around, and I was thrown against another huge rock.

By then, I had lost my paddle and all I could do was scream as another swirl of water whipped the canoe around so hard I nearly fell out! I was just hanging on to the sides of the canoe. And then the water around me was suddenly quiet, but I could hear, ahead of me, the roaring rapids, louder and louder, and then I was looking at a three-foot drop of foaming, swirling, deafening falls! I could do nothing but hang on!

I screamed as the canoe pitched forward and then suddenly whipped about so fast that the next thing I knew, I was thrown from the canoe and felt water bub-

bling in my ears as I went under. Huge claws of water grabbed hold of me and, as hard as I could struggle, I couldn't move as I was thrown very hard against a rock.

The force knocked the wind out of me and I choked on water. Hacking and coughing, I was thrown like a sack of flour from one rock to another, until I literally slid over the final rock and found myself going around and around in a little pool. My flying hands met some branches and my left hand managed to clamp down on them before I was sucked under the current again.

I hung on, in a big fight to haul my body away from the pull of the water. I flailed away with my feet, but the current kept pushing them to the surface so that I couldn't stand up to get a footing. I managed to grab the branch with both hands and hoped that it would hold. My body was still being swung left and right on the upper current of water.

After what felt like an eternity, I managed to move my hands up higher on the overhanging tree, until I had fished my body away from the grasp of the current. Finally, in total exhaustion, I felt my feet touch bottom. My knees shook so badly I could hardly stand up. My fingers ached and my whole body felt like I had been whipped over and over against a rock, which I guess is exactly what had happened.

I slowly dragged my aching body, one step at a time, to the shore and sat down on the mossy bank. I could not hear from one ear. I knew it was full of water. I felt sticky blood oozing from my arms, elbows, knees, legs, and the pain on my chin told me it was also scraped raw.

I sat there for the longest time, until I became aware that I should start moving and getting away from there. I stood on shaky legs and pulled myself onto dry ground. It was dark now, and I wasn't sure which way to go. The flies were buzzing around everywhere. Soon, the mosquitoes would find me. I looked around, trying to figure out where to step, but I couldn't see anything.

There was no help for it, I would have to blindly stumble around and hope to reach solid, even ground. I reasoned that if the river flowed north, then I would have to turn to head south to get back upriver. Then I would only have to follow the sound of the river on my left and I would be on the same shoreline as the camp. That was logical.

I set about groping through the darkness. I followed the higher ground to avoid the swamp and mosquitoes, and besides, it was better walking here. It was relatively smooth over rock and moss. I also discovered with dismay that I had only one sock on. Both my shoes were gone and my right sock was gone too. I had no idea where the canoe was or at what point I had left the river.

I groped from branch to branch, moving as quickly as I could in the darkness. I could no longer hear the river and there was no sign of a shoreline up ahead either. My feet began to get very sore. I slowed down and realized that I might not be going in a straight line! In renewed fear, I realized it was possible that I would have to spend the night here in the bush all by myself!

Almost in a panic, I started walking faster and faster, through the pain, and then began to run. Suddenly, I tripped. On my way down, a broken branch left a big scratch across my eyebrow that just missed my eye! My hand came away sticky-bloody as I brushed my hand over my face. Oh, my gosh! I started bawling my eyes out.

I cried and cried and then, just as suddenly, I stopped. I realized that if I was that loud, a bear could hear me and know I was wounded and in pain. He would come and eat me! That's what bears did. Didn't they? Hitz said so. My heart was pounding very loudly in my ears as I sat there wondering what to do next. My ear was still plugged, which amplified the pounding of my heart. Well, I would have to patch myself up and make like I knew what I was doing and was in total control of the situation. That way the bear would not come close. I hoped.

I felt the trees around me. There were tamarack trees and pine trees. There was a bit of mossy ground over to the left and rockier, higher ground to my right. I couldn't see anything at all now, and I could feel the coolness of the night. What to do next? Blood was coming down my face and oozing from my knees and elbows. I felt back to the tamarack tree. What had Grandma said about the bark? I bit into a branch and scratched with my nails until I got some of the sticky brown stuff on my fingers and this I smeared on my eyebrow. After the initial sting, the blood seemed to stop. I did the same to my elbow and knees. Now that I felt sufficiently patched up, I hobbled over to the pine trees and broke off branches. I got a whole bunch of them stacked up, I hoped more or less in the same spot, since I could not see what I was doing.

I felt around and laid the branches in a circle and then, by twisting some around the bushes and putting some more branches on top of that, I figured I had got some overhead shelter as well as around the sides. I curled up in the soft middle part of my shelter and pulled as many branches as I could on top of me. As much as I was afraid, I had no sooner put my head down and listened to the singing of the mosquitoes, than I went right to sleep.

I awoke quite early in the morning. The mosquitoes had found my legs and feet. There was nothing I could do to keep them off me. So I sat curled up under a tree by my makeshift shelter, which I now saw was pretty poorly done, for sure. The roof and sides I thought I'd constructed were no more than a few branches sprawled on the ground around the pile of branches that I never actually slept on!

I sat fanning the mosquitoes away from me with one of the pine branches. I had no idea which way was home. I couldn't figure out why I had not come across to the other side of the shore. As I sat there with my arms over my knees and my head resting on my arms, I must have fallen asleep again, for when I woke up, the sun was just coming up...from the west? Why was the sun coming up from the west?

I knelt down on the ground, pushed away the moss, and picked up a stick. If I was going up the river along the west shore toward camp – with the shore to the east away from camp – why was the sun coming up in the west?

I sat stunned for a long two minutes before I realized what I had done! I had been on the east side and walked north away from the rapids, thinking I was on the west side going south, towards camp! Now, I must be almost a good...what? A mile down the river away from camp! Dumb! Dumb! Dumb! I was so angry with myself, I punched my leg hard, then realized I would have to limp on that too! I got up and walked quickly to where I thought the edge of the river should be and, sure enough, the sound of the river became louder. Soon, I scrambled up the east side of the river bank.

Wait a minute! Two guys had just come out of the portage and set their canoe down on the landing. Those were the guys from the group camped next to us. I yelled and waved, "Hey! Hey!" Where was Grandma's canoe? By now, Grandma must be going crazy! Oh, Dummy! Dummy! Dummy! I said to myself as I scrambled down to the water's edge.

I could see the men coming, paddling very fast towards me. I followed the shoreline up the river, skipping along the shore of the rapids where I could, and I soon recognized the place where I had finally reached shore. There was still no sign of the canoe. I crawled over more logs and toppled-over trees and went around swamps, until I finally came to a quieter pool of water.

Then the men reached me. The man at the front jumped out of the canoe and grabbed my arm to steady me into their canoe, asking, "What on earth are you doing here?"

I yelled over the sound of the river, "I got swept over the rapids last night. I don't know where Grandma's canoe went!"

After I was settled in the middle of the canoe, they turned toward the reed-filled bay beyond the mouth of the river and there, nudging the shoreline, was the canoe, still upright. The man at the front reached out to the canoe and pulled it to us. It did not seem any the worse for wear. I guess after it dumped me, it sailed down the rapids quite quickly.

I searched the shoreline for the paddle, but it was nowhere in sight. Just then, the man at the back said, "Your paddle is over there by the weeds." He was pointing somewhere at the bay behind me. They looked at each other and started laughing. I didn't think it was a laughing matter at all.

After a short conference, they said, "We were just out to check our fishnet over there, but we'll take your canoe back up the portage and then you can paddle back to camp. Your grandma is still with Sarah, so you can be home and she won't know any better, okay?"

I nodded, but somehow that didn't seem right. But right now, I wasn't going to argue. They had the canoe back up the portage in no time and I yelled, "Thanks!" over the roar of the river. They waved and I got slowly back into Grandma's canoe. My cuts and bruises were really hurting still. It took me about fifteen minutes to paddle back to the campsite, during which I thought of a half dozen or more excuses and explanations and none sounded good at all.

When I finally got the canoe back where it was supposed to be, I pulled it up and turned it over on the soft cedar trees. It didn't seem to have suffered damage, except for a new scratch toward the middle – maybe that was where it had hit the rock that threw me overboard. It was a fibreglass canoe and I was relatively light in it, so it looked like I was in a whole lot worse shape than that little canoe was.

I walked, or rather limped, up the sloping rock and slowly made my way to the tent, almost dreading to see the smoke from the campfire. But as I came to the clearing, there was the campsite, with still no smoke and no sign of life. I hurried forward now. It was breakfast time and I was starving! I grabbed some wood as I entered the clearing and got the fire going. I was getting concerned for Grandma now too. She had been gone an awful long time. I wondered if things were all right.

After rummaging around in the food box, I decided to make macaroni, which I boiled in a pot at the campfire, and then I diced some bologna and dumped it into the strained macaroni with a can of tomatoes. I had just mixed the whole thing together over the fire when I saw her slowly make her way around the rocks along the beach.

She looked very tired, but she had a wide grin on her face as she came up to the fire. "It's a boy!" she exclaimed. "Oh, I tell you! He is a really big boy! Really worked us into the ground, that boy! She says she's gonna call him Hercules! I told her to call him Devilis!"

I smiled, said nothing, and dished out a big plate of food for her. Just then, I noticed her stop and examine me from top to bottom. She said, "So, tell me what was the thing that dragged you through the forest, bush, and mud to make you look like that?" I snorted in my unexpected giggle.

After we had settled down beside the fire with a plate of food each, I decided to tell her exactly what I had done since the time she left the campsite the day before. She wrinkled a face at me but continued to munch at her meal. Finally she said, "You know, this is quite good! But do tell me that you have learned a lesson and that you will never take the canoe again without telling me, okay?"

I nodded. "Yes, Grandma. I promise I will never take the canoe again without asking, and if I do, I will tell you exactly where I'm going and at what time I'll return." She kicked the wood piece I was sitting on so hard, I spun around and found myself facing the bush.

BACK HOME

I HATED GOING BACK HOME. I HELD GRANDMA'S HAND AS we stood by the station waiting for the train to come. We said nothing as we watched the crowd growing around the station and down to the general store. The train engine's headlight appeared around the curve. I felt Grandma's hand tighten around mine, but she said nothing as she picked up my suitcase and handed it to me. As the train came to a stop, I hugged Grandma, and my chest ached so bad I thought I was going to burst something inside me. I turned and climbed up the steps of the train. After the first immense pain when the train left the station and Portage One and Two went by, my pain became the one familiar dull ache. It was back. I sat looking outside the window and never said a thing to anybody on the way home. Even my brain didn't feel like talking. I just watched the telephone poles go marching by the train window, mile after mile.

When the train arrived at home, I got off and had to walk home with my suitcase over my shoulder. I figured it took me almost half an hour before I finally turned into our little walkway. The window was dark, so I knew they had already gone to bed. Slowly, I walked up the narrow walkway and pushed the door open, and there was Mama hunched over the table.

What was the matter? I dropped my suitcase and hurried forward and touched her shoulder. "Mama, are you okay?"

She jumped and exclaimed, "Oh, goodness! Ray! I was going to walk down the road to meet you! I must have fallen asleep. Oh, I'm so sorry, baby! Here I was, waiting for the time I thought it would take for you to get to the corner and I would meet you there!"

She held me so tight against her as she spoke against my ear, that I began to think there was really something wrong. I asked, "Cindy and Billy okay?"

"Oh, yes. They've been in bed for a long time. Everything's fine. It's just that I've missed you so much. You don't realize, but I depend on you a lot. You know, watching things and making sure everything's okay with them...anyway, I am so happy you're home safe and sound. Did you have fun?"

I smiled. "Yes, Mama. I had a lot of fun and I learned a lot of things too. Thank you for letting me stay with Grandma."

I didn't know what else to say. There was so much I

wanted to say, like it would have been nice to have her with us to watch the sunsets in the evening and the early morning orange tinge in the sky just beneath an over-hanging dark cloud...but there just were no words for things like that. My mind was so much better at speaking about things of that sort. My lips and mind just didn't seem to coordinate when I was back here.

I just hugged her a bit and got ready for bed as she went about locking the door and banking up the stove for the night.

As the months passed, we went about our regular schedules again, going through the motions of living day to day. At first I really tried to make an effort to talk to Mama, because she was always harping at me to talk to her, but more and more I felt myself just shutting down. I absolutely hated living in this town! I went to school, came home, did my homework, and went with weary heart and dreaded steps back to school every morning. But always in my mind was Grandma and her warm, happy, cozy little cabin. Mama did her best to cheer me up, but I was just too busy feeling sorry for myself, I guess.

I did odd jobs here and there to earn some money. I babysat for some people in the neighbourhood and for Charlie and his wife. I would go around on the weekends to see if anyone would pay me to help them out. But I was not interested in the people themselves. I only wanted some money to add to my savings.

I was so intent on trying to find ways to make money that I think I even went for a week one time without saying a word at home. I didn't even notice until one morning when Mama parked herself in front of the door after Billy and Cindy had gone out and demanded I talk to her. I just shrugged and wondered what she was talking about. What did she want me to say to her?

I had nothing to say. There was nothing happening in my life that I needed to share with anybody. There was nothing I could plan ahead for. There was nothing to hope for. There was nothing even to think about!

So, in a mournful, pleading, beseeching voice, Mama stood in front of me and said, "Talk to me, baby. Ray, say something! What is the matter?" I just stood there, raised my eyebrows, screwed my lips, and shrugged.

"Hi. How are you doing? I'm doing fine. Isn't it a nice day today?" I meant to be funny, but she looked so hurt. She looked at me for another minute before she heaved a big sigh and gave me a big hug and I ran out to catch up with Billy and Cindy. I didn't glance back at the cabin, although I knew Mama would be standing at the door, watching us going down the street and around the bend.

It was around the middle of October and school dragged on as it always did. The kids snickering at what I was wearing and just dying to see what I had brought for lunch. That was their pastime, finding things to make fun of me with for the rest of the day. That morning, the lesson began with moose. I did a lot of reading and constantly took books home with me. Well, I had read somewhere that moose ate "succulent greens" in the bays during the summer months when the flies drove them into the water. So, when the teacher had finished talking about how the moose calves were born in the spring and how they would feed with their mothers in the creeks and bays, he asked a question:

"What is it that they would be eating?"

Well, in my once-a-year incentive to answer a question, I stuck my arm up in the air. You'd think it had actually hit the ceiling, the response it got from the students. The teacher made a slow, deliberate concentration on my very own important self, to answer the one very important question of the whole universe, and I answered in a soft voice.

"The succulent greens, sir."

Well, needless to say, there was an uproar of "Succulent Greens!" "Succulent Ray!" "Succulent Greens for Succulent Green Eyes!" Even at lunch, as I sat in the corner hunched over my bannock and Klik sandwich, some of the boys were still yelling, "Hey, how much for succulent greens, Ray?" I put them down in my "Stupid Idiots" shelf and finished my sandwich in peace.

Then I opened my mouth one more time in class that afternoon and it landed me in trouble.

Finally, the bell rang and school was over for the day.

I heaved a big sigh of relief and stood outside in the late afternoon sun before I got my feet to move. I could not for the life of me see what it was all about. Why were they making me go through all this? Would I be going on like this all the rest of my life? That was a very seriously depressing thought!

At what point would I be able to take control of my life? When would I be able to do what I would like to do? If I couldn't ever do that, then what was the point? I just didn't understand. When was this "forced school" stuff supposed to end? Oh, I was in one huge miserable mood that day.

You see, I was the last to get out of school, because I was forced to wait for a very long time for the principal to finish whatever he was doing before he got around to dealing with me. When I finally sat down in front of him and the secretary told him what I was sent in to see him for, he just stared at me like he really, really hated me. I still didn't get the point, for all I had said was, "A person should not be talking about something he doesn't know anything about."

But what did it matter? I just stared at the principal and said nothing at all. He said, between his very clenched teeth, "I want to hear no more of this, do you hear me? You are never to say such things to the teacher again!"

I nodded. So that was what this was about. Some boys beside me had been saying something about me when I'd responded. I guess the teacher thought I was talking to him. I didn't even hear what he'd said, because I was busy listening to the boys.

Anyway, I was out the door, wondering what the principal would actually do if I did it again. I pulled my cap down farther around my ears. I had decided to put my beaver-skin cap on this morning. I didn't care what the kids called me, you couldn't beat the warmth and it didn't disturb your hairstyle. I mean, it didn't clamp your hair down flat like other hats. It actually pulled the hair up to a plump bounce when you pulled it off. It was my father's beaver-skin hat, and I liked it just fine!

Just as I had stomped my feet across the road to the little path that ran parallel to the muddy parts and as I was ready to burst into tears, I noticed Hitz coming at a very slow walk. I stopped and waited. He stopped, sniffed a big breath, lifted his shaggy toque-topped head and looked at the sky, and said, "H'it's going to be very cold tonight. Might be some snow coming soon."

I too looked up and nodded. His rubber boots squeaked as they adjusted to get a better grip of the road. His pants still looked like they were ready to take off at a fast run, the knees protruding for a steady jaunt. I smiled.

Then he said, "You're late. Why...why you going home so late for?"

I shrugged and my soft voice said, "I said something back to the boys and the teacher thought I was talking to him." Anyway, what did it matter!

I shrugged my shoulders. Hitz took another upward heave of breath, sucking up his shoulders along with it, before his one rubber boot shot out and just as quickly, he sidestepped me and I nodded as he shuffled on by.

I walked on slowly, wishing I was back with my grandma. I knew Billy and Cindy would probably be home by now, but I dragged my feet. That was when I remembered a new book I had taken out of the library that afternoon! I now hurried to get home. The book was about giant snakes of the Amazon forest.

Just as I came to the bend of the gravel road, I smelled the smoke. Smoke like...tar and then more like wood. I began to run. I smelled more tar and wood together. By the time I rounded the bend, I knew for sure that our little house was burning! I screamed as I ran around the trees to the walkway. I saw that our whole cabin was on fire! The whole thing was burning!

I saw Mama struggling with two guys. She wanted to run inside the cabin, which was already engulfed in flames! Suddenly, Billy was right there beside her and I knew it was Cindy who must still be there in the cabin! I lunged forward, and just as Mama gave a final gouge and kick at the man beside her and was hurling herself at the front door, I clamped my arms around her.

We fell to the ground and I held her there, and she finally became still under me as I screamed, "Mama! Mama! Mama!" over the noise of the fire, people, police, and the fire engine. Then she started a howl of anguish that I had never heard in my whole life! She screamed, screeched, and moaned like a strange human in some horrid movie and I found my own voice joining hers.

I screamed and cried as I had never done before! I still had her pinned underneath me and now we just held each other as I gradually rolled to her side. She kissed my forehead as she cried, and I too hugged and kissed her between my screams of anguish.

Suddenly, a fireman rushed up beside us, saying that they didn't believe there was anyone else inside...then we heard, "Mama! Mama!" There was Cindy! We scrambled up and ran to the line of people where she had just materialized. She had apparently been next door with the farm chickens. We were all safe! We fell to our knees and clutched at each other as we watched our little house go down in flames.

Just then, Charlie showed up beside us, and he grabbed Mama and crushed her to his chest, and he rocked her side to side for the longest time, while I held Billy and Cindy on each side of me. Finally, Charlie stood up and began kissing Mama on the face and I noticed that she was struggling to push him back. Then he gathered us together and ushered us toward his truck.

There was nothing left of the little house now and the men from the fire truck just milled about. The police had finished talking to Mama and the other people who had stopped and were now going on their way. Charlie piled us into his truck and we headed to his place. As always,

Mama rode in the truck with Charlie and the three of us scampered into the back.

Charlie's wife was at the door when we all came up the walk behind him. She didn't say anything, but swung the door open and headed for the kitchen. They had three children, aged four, six, and eight. Two girls and Jonathan. I didn't mind babysitting them, they were nice little girls, and Jonathan was never around anyway. We crammed into the kitchen with their girls as Mama, Charlie, and Milly sat talking in the other room. Then Charlie came in and told us we would occupy the children's room for the time being and Jonathan and their girls would bunk out in their room, as there were only two bedrooms in the house.

I hugged Billy and Cindy and told them everything was going to be all right. I had babysat for these people many times and their kids were okay. But I did not volunteer anything about Milly. She was very mean to me and always pretended I was not there. I knew it was Charlie who hired me to babysit their kids if they had to go somewhere. I figured he knew I could use the money, and that was why he was always there to pick me up and take me back home again. Charlie was a very nice man.

It was not until the next day that the outcome of the fire hit me. We stayed with Charlie and Milly that one day and I knew right away that it was not going to work! There was something very wrong between Charlie, Milly, and Mama, and you could feel the tension, but I didn't ask and Mama didn't tell me.

All our clothes and food had been burnt in the fire, but the townspeople were very good in their charity. We got clothes to wear to school. Mama got kitchen stuff and a bit of clothing, but what really hurt me most of all was...I mean I was very thankful that none of my family got hurt, but you see, I lost all my hard-earned money I had saved from babysitting, sweeping driveways, cleaning yards, mowing lawns, and taking care of gardens for the old people for many months. I had almost saved enough money to see Grandma at Easter. I'd had all the dollars and change saved under my bed. Now it was all gone!

The next day, when we came back from school, Mama told us we had another home to go to. This house was just up the hill from the other school and it was a flat log cabin. It was the home of someone Mama and Father had met some years ago. The man had two boys and they lived in one half of the house, leaving a vacant two-bedroom half. That was where we would live for the time being, until something better came up. So the man, Dave, came and picked us up, along with the odds and ends of donations that had been left at the door. We left Charlie's place, with Mama thanking Milly for taking us in. Then we waited for Mama to get into the truck beside the driver. That was the last time we saw Charlie and Milly for a long time. They never asked me to babysit for them after that.

We arrived at Dave's low log cabin late in the evening. It didn't look very inviting. It was way on the edge of town and there was nothing after that but bush. We got out of the truck and hesitantly went into the house. There in the middle of the kitchen stood Henry and Todd. They were introduced to us as Dave's eight- and ten-year-old sons. They began to scramble about to make us feel at home. I got the impression that they were just starved for company!

That night when I was able to sneak into Mama's room, I scrambled into bed with her and asked how she had come to know this man. She said she had heard about him many years before Father died. His wife had died at the birth of their baby son. That was eight years ago, I thought. Dave was Father's friend and he'd had supper at our place several times, but I didn't remember him. But since Father's death, he had been a good friend to Mama and he had apparently delivered some extra food for us, in between the cheques, that Mama had decided not to mention to us. Anyway, so now here we were, in his house.

The boys seemed nice. Certainly, Billy was in kid heaven at discovering boys to play with. I was concerned about Cindy, though. But as the weeks went by, Cindy became the little sister for all the boys and discovered a new identity. I, on the other hand, faced my mother wondering what this arrangement was going to come to. Mama had also told me that Charlie wasn't likely to ask me to babysit anymore. She'd told him he wasn't to bother her anymore. It appeared that Charlie loved her, but she had never wanted anything to do with him in that way.

After a month, we had all things organized and a routine of some sort set up, so that we did not have to wait on each other. When Christmas came, we had a wonderful time, and we discovered Dave and the two boys had a regular Christmas thing going every year. They had all kinds of Christmas decorations all over the place and a Christmas tree in the corner of the living room. We got to eat a huge turkey and all the trimmings, and we each had a gift under the Christmas tree. That was the happiest Christmas we had ever had since Father died. But I still missed Grandma. I wanted so much to sit beside her and just listen to her breathing and feel her soft hand on mine. You could rub the backs of her hands and her skin would wrinkle into waves like the surface of the water and then disappear again.

The new school was nice. There were many Native students in my class and they seemed to know what was going on. I never once felt like I was put down or like I was just dirt. The teacher was actually interested in knowing about things that he obviously didn't know anything about.

One day at school in the springtime, in our geography class, an old Native man came into our class to explain how the plants were used for medicinal purposes. In our history class, guess who came into our class? Ol'

Hitz! There he was describing how beaver traps and all kinds of other traps were set in the summer, spring, winter, and fall! When he was finished, he gave a very wide toothless smile at me! That was so wonderful! I was just busting to get home that day to tell Mama about Hitz in class. But when I arrived home, Billy, Cindy, Henry, and Todd were already in the living room diving for popcorn balls Mama had made for a snack before supper.

I had just come into the porch, and for the first time, I stood smiling at the happy scene in front of me. Then I heard Dave behind me. I ducked inside the porch and turned to see who he was speaking to. I couldn't see, so I moved into the living room with the rest of the kids and waited to see who Dave was coming home with.

Well, Mama was sitting on the couch, Cindy was trying to clip some new suspenders on Billy, and Henry and Todd were still arguing about the roll of toilet paper that suddenly disappeared from behind a girl's desk at school. The idea, as far as I could figure out, was that someone was supposed to stick the end of the toilet paper to the top elastic of her skirt and "just let it roll" when she got up. Well, needless to say, it didn't work.

Anyway, there was a commotion in the porch and then Dave entered with his moose gun held in front of him. He had apparently gone hunting that morning and now here he was, very late in the day. As soon as he was inside and set the rifle down in the hallway and removed the bullets, his companion came into the living room behind him. There, plain as you please, stood a very long-legged, nervous, baby moose!

"I was just coming home from not seeing anything in sight," Dave said, "when I got the feeling that someone was following me. So, I'd stop and slowly turn around... there was no one. Then I would walk a ways down the path again and I'd feel the person coming along behind me again, so I'd stop and look back. Still, no one. Finally, I ran on ahead and ducked behind a stump and turned to look back and there...comes this lost and lonely baby moose. He maybe thought I was his mama. Anyway, there was no way I could get rid of him. I tried chasing him away, calling him all kinds of names, and even threw dirt and branches at him...but here he is."

At this point, he bowed and waved the moose on in front of us, like some dashing knight at a queen's court! We broke out in giggles as the baby moose nuzzled him behind the ear. That was the strangest thing I had ever seen in my whole life! A baby moose in a living room, nuzzling against a Native hunter!

Suddenly, Mama set up a screech! "Get a pail, get a shovel, get a basin, get a tub, anything!"

By this time, we could see that the baby moose had decided to go for a big long pee right in the middle of the living room! First, Todd showed up with the slop pail, but the moose was moving to catch up with Dave. Then Henry showed up with a small washtub, but the moose was still moving. Finally, Billy showed up with a big shovel and managed to catch the last of the pee before Mama was there to head the moose off, and then Dave and Mama managed to turn it around. They tried pushing it back out the door, but the baby moose kept turning to the left and to the right.

In the meantime, Cindy and the boys were laughing their heads off. It really was a funny sight – Mama chasing the back end of the baby moose and Dave trying to push its head away and steer it to the door. Mother yelled, "Dave, stop moving!" Dave stopped and together they turned the moose around, faced him in the direction of the door that I was holding open, and finally managed to push him out the door.

Dave went out and built a little lean-to outside for the moose, while we got a can of condensed milk. The baby moose licked it all up in really big slurps. Then we set out a basin of water. He drank that up too. Then Cindy yelled, "What does he eat, Ray?" My mind immediately said, "Succulent greens!"

It was several days before the Ministry of Natural Resources managed to come and get the baby moose and ship him to another location where he would not venture into town again.

Charlie dropped by one day when Dave was not home and told Mama that he and a group of men were coming home through a clear-cut logging site when they spotted two bear cubs. Well, the cubs came running up to them like they hadn't eaten in quite awhile, so they fed the baby bears all the sandwiches they had left. When the babies had swallowed the last bit, suddenly a huge form rose behind them and roared like, well, you would not want to hear that, so they all scrambled back to the trucks and took off! We all laughed. But I got the impression that this was not what he had come to tell us. We ran off and left him to talk to Mama. Later, I happened to pass by the corner of the house and they were still by the driveway talking, and then I saw Mama and Charlie shaking hands.

Coming home rather late the next afternoon, I slowed down and watched Dave hard at work. He was dumping gravel down the driveway to cover up the mudholes that we would all eventually track into the house for Mama to yell at us about. I watched him push the wheelbarrow full of gravel up the driveway and to the door.

I stopped to look at him for the first time. His black curly hair had a way of tucking itself neatly at the edge of his collar and also lay neatly around his face and temples. I had never seen a Native man look so well groomed in my whole life. He was a very muscular man, his arms and legs as big around as...Father's had been. My mind immediately scampered onto other things. I saw that the blue jays had finally found our seeds and suet! But, no. He was not going to let me get away.

Dave walked right toward me and stopped just two inches from my face.

He said, "Ray. My dear girl, I understand this has been very hard on you. You can believe me when I say I understand because I...I may as well be standing right where you are now...."

I stepped back and stared at him. What on earth was he talking about?

"I lost my father and then I got a stepfather," he continued. "I just want to tell you right now that I want all you children to be my own. I want to marry your mother – oh, by the way, I haven't even asked her yet!" He chuckled and kicked at the dirt before he glanced up at me almost as if he was pleading with me.

"Ray. You see, I can't do this if I don't have your support. So, as strange as it may sound to you, here is my proposition." He went into the Shakespearean bow of a knight in a lady's court, swept off his invisible befeathered hat, and asked:

"Will you, Lady Ray, allow me to wed your beloved mother?"

Quite surprising myself, I made a gesture of batting aside his hand and held up a finger against his chin. "Sir, you may wed my mother, providing you never do an ungentlemanly thing for the rest of your days. If you do, I shall have my knight slay you without mercy!"

He fell back onto the steps and sat there with a hand over his throat. "Who is this knight that would slay me?"

I stood over him and said, "Why, my faithful servant, Hitz, sir! He would slay you on the spot!"

He was rolling in helpless giggles when Mama came up from around the side of the house. I hurried inside and left Dave to explain. I knew for sure Mama would never, ever, believe I would do such a thing. I had discovered that I could do one thing that was expected of me, then turn around and do something totally different, so that it became impossible for people who hadn't witnessed my acts to believe they actually happened.

I glanced outside from the living room window to see Mama look up at the house with a bewildered expression and then shake her head in wonder. Was she contemplating Dave's proposal? Or maybe Dave had just told her what I'd said. It was weird, but it was Dave who introduced us to the world of Kings, Queens, Princes, Princesses, Knights, and Ladies. I loved it! He would read from a stack of books on his desk by the window near the stove. Mama said he was very over-educated for the job he was doing at the Forestry office.

That evening, it didn't come as a big surprise to me when Mama and Dave announced that they were going to get married in the fall. But I was surprised at the sense of anger that first swept through me at the thought of my father being "replaced." Then a gradual acceptance settled over me. I decided that my father would want my mother to marry, so that my younger brother and sister could have a father – since I was beginning to doubt whether they remembered him at all! That really hurt too. But they were too small. Too young to remember.

I decided that if I was going to have a stepfather, Mama could not have picked a better man than Dave. I liked him. I liked the way he talked to me, the way he asked about things that might matter to me. I...I guess I just liked him, that's all.

The boys were so excited, but Cindy, for some strange reason, said nothing at all. Suddenly, the house took on an air of excitement and the boys moved our brother in with them in their room and Cindy and I shared the other room. Mama still had her room, now crammed with a sewing machine and boxes of used clothing and material. Everyday, she sat sewing new clothes for us or cutting the donated clothes down to size to fit us.

There was one dress in particular that she held up to me, exclaiming how beautiful it would look on me. I noticed that it could fit her, so I said, "Try it on, Mama."

"Oh, no. I don't need a dress like this. When would I wear such a thing?"

I smiled and whispered, "On special days when Dave is home and you cook those nice meals, or when you go out sometimes...." I noticed that her face had turned red. I looked away and busied myself doing something else. I turned to see that she had folded it nicely and set it aside on the bed.

Finally, school was over and the boys skipped and hooted with joy as they took off into the bush behind the house to the treehouse they had built back there. It was out of bounds for me and, as they often exclaimed, "Especially Cindy!" As a result, Cindy spent a lot of time with Mama, and I went about my usual business, working at odd jobs for people to make a little money. Over the winter, I had almost accumulated the same amount as I had lost in the fire. I needed a few dollars more and I would have enough for a ticket to see Grandma!

As it turned out, I came home one day and I saw the truck outside and Dave inside in the living room. He was not supposed to be home that early, but there he was. He handed me an envelope. Quite puzzled, I took it and flipped it open. There inside...was a ticket to Grandma's! I laughed and hugged it to me and then the realization hit that I could go, right now! All Dave said was, "You have half an hour to pack your stuff and I already called your grandma. She'll be waiting for you when you get there."

I had already whirled around to run for my things when I caught Mother's eye, oh yes. I turned back to Dave to say thank you, but quite unexpectedly, so that I even surprised myself, I threw my arms around his chest and said, "Thank you, Dave." His arms closed around me...hard muscular arms...suddenly Father came crashing into my head! I jerked back really fast and stood there rather confused for a second, before I managed to smile and nod at Dave and then I took off to my room.

We just made it to the train station and then I was on the train, waving goodbye to them all as they crowded around by the side of the railroad tracks. I sat down on the seat and the train lurched forward.

GRANDMA'S PLACE
SUMMER 1980

I STEPPED OFF THE TRAIN AND THERE SHE WAS. SHE HAD her little black tam smack on top of her head. Underneath that tam, I knew she had braided hair from both sides of her head pinned to the top, over which the tam was pulled down to her ears. She beamed a big smile. She had shiny white teeth, which she always made mention of whenever she told me I couldn't have any candy. Her wrinkled cheeks stretched to her eyes as she smiled and giggled, giving me a big hug.

She wore the black sweater buttoned only on the top button over a homemade blouse, which I knew she made simply with a hem across a flat front with gathered sleeves. Her skirt was gathered at the waist and flowed to the hem above her shoes. I held her as if my life depended on it until she started to laugh and pulled my arms down. The train started with a loud hissing and grunting as the huge steel wheels began to move again.

There were many other people standing around the train station waiting for someone or just curious about who was getting off. I loved the place! There was a wide open field of grass and there were no streets or cars. Poplar trees banked the clearing where the station and the only general store stood. From there, paths splayed out in all directions. When the train disappeared around the bend, we walked along the railway tracks, hand in hand.

I carried my suitcase and we walked along without talking. I glanced at Grandma occasionally and we smiled at each other. There was no need for words. It was a lovely July afternoon. Everything was quiet as we watched the butterflies fluttering amongst the flowers and the grasshoppers hopping amongst the bushes.

I walked with my suitcase bumping along the side of my leg. Just then, the silence – the absolute peaceful serenity of the place – hit me. I paused and took a deep breath. Grandma stood beside me when I stopped, but said not a word. When I moved again, I was surprised to find that tears were rolling down my face! I let the tears roll and drip down my chin and into my throat but I made no noise. I felt Grandma's arm come across my shoulder, holding me close.

I noticed a squirrel scampering up a rock pile. He came to a stop on top, looked directly at us, and gave a huge indignant chatter about all the noise we had no business making! I smiled and whispered, "Sorry, Chitamoo. But this is the way to Grandma's home. Where is yours?"

The squirrel scampered off the rock and with a parting shot at us, he disappeared amongst the rocks.

Grandma laughed softly and said, "Naens, my Little Voice, you just uttered a Great Voice today. You have learned a lot."

I spotted the path and we scrambled off the tracks in cascading showers of gravel, then headed into the bushes, following the trail. It was cool in the shade. Grandma pointed at some thick blueberry bushes.

"Look over there, that is a good bunch for blueberry bannock some morning," she said. "Oh, later in the fall, before you go, look there! There's going to be loads and loads of pin cherries there. They make a wonderful jam for fried bannock!"

As we got closer to the cabin, she pointed to some chokecherry bushes covered with clusters of shiny red berries. "I tell you, this summer is going to be very good for berries! We will pick baskets and baskets of blueberries for your mother and aunties this summer!" I said nothing as I followed her. It was so wonderful to hear her voice. She spoke only Ojibwa.

"Oh, I even got a bunch of moss cranberries all frozen – in the storekeeper's freezer. Don't you tell anybody that. He's got a secret deal with me not to tell anybody." She turned, smiling, and added, "It is only because I have to give him a basket of those cranberries for Thanksgiving, Christmas, New Years, and Easter. Can't beat the wild cranberries for that!"

As always, when Mama or Grandma was telling me something, I remained silent and listened and remembered everything that was said. If my opinion was required, they would ask me, but then it was most likely a "test question." You were left to wonder if it was the right or wrong answer, because it was left up to you to learn. So, if you were wrong with your response, time and experience would correct your wrong answer. You were supposed to learn on our own and at your own speed, figuring things out yourself.

As I walked behind her soft, low-heeled shoes, I stopped to observe the things she noticed and hurried when I got sidetracked with other things that she took no notice of, and pretty soon we entered a clearing. And there was her little cabin, the same as it had always been – undisturbed, quiet, and peaceful. I heaved a big sigh and took a big breath of air and even took the urge to spread my arms out wide!

"What was that about? You just let a bird go, or what?"

I laughed. "I guess I did. I really did feel like I just let a caged bird go free! Off and away it went!" Grandma paused, waiting for more, but I could think of nothing else to say. Just then, we were at her doorstep.

I nudged at her flower bed by the door and said, "I thought you were going to plant some exotic flowers there this spring."

She shrugged. "Couldn't be bothered after the kids

went and ripped out my tulips from the flower bed on the other side of the walkway."

Oh, yes. The kids. I could not understand why they did that. Weren't they curious what kinds of flowers would come from the seeds and bulbs Grandma planted? I think they were probably daring each other who would have the nerve to destroy Grandma's flowers.

Grandma found a large fresh pike lying in the washtub outside when we arrived. Someone had left it there for her while she had gone to meet me at the station. I had found that strange last summer when people brought food to Grandma from time to time. It could be moose meat, rabbits, partridge, or fish. If she wasn't home, they just left it somewhere by the door. Most of the time, she had no idea who had left the food.

The sun was just setting now and we brought in enough wood to last the night. Grandma had scraped the scales off the fish and gutted it, but before she could get the fire going again, a neighbour showed up at the door. It was Joshua, an old man who lived way out to the west of Grandma's cabin. I mean, I had thought Grandma's was the last house at the west side of the community, but tucked way out, against the hillside, was Joshua's cabin.

Joshua didn't come into the community very often, but here he was. He gave a big toothless grin at Grandma and handed over a red blood-encrusted piece of meat. Grandma showed great surprise and even uttered a laugh as he came in and deposited his gift into a bowl she pulled out from a bottom shelf. Our fish went into Joshua's hand and we got the meat.

Grandma took the meat outside and I could hear them talking in Ojibwa. I realized that their conversation was different than the way Grandma talked to me. I heard them laughing in between the silences of unspoken words. I found myself smiling. Joshua had a soft, slow, wheezing laugh, like someone who was not used to laughing very often. After spending the time with Grandma last summer, my Ojibwa was much better now, but not as good as what I was listening to.

Needless to say, we were eating meat, along with the fish, for Joshua was now invited to eat with us. I immediately felt resentful that I had to spend my first night with Grandma with another person I didn't even know! I dumped out my clothes on the other single bed in Grandma's cabin and piled my clothes along the wall.

I pulled out the teapot from the top shelf as I was used to doing. There was no water, and I knew that I should not need to be asked to go fetch it. I grabbed the bucket and ran toward the creek without looking back. I slowed down as I entered the muddy, swampy area by the creek.

It was evening now and the butterflies fluttered about the swamp flowers. I slowed down to a very slow walk and wandered to the boat landing. The evening sun was now slanting over the trees, casting an orange tint over the trees and bushes. Little blue dragonflies flittered over the plants on the shoreline. I stood and breathed another great big sigh. I looked out into the bay and out to the open water beyond. Everything was very quiet and peaceful. Dogs were barking somewhere to the east of the community and it gave a very calming presence to my surroundings.

Suddenly, my eyes flooded with tears, and I could not understand why, but I went down on my knees and sobbed as I had not done in what seemed like ages. Every fibre of my being gushed out as I leaned out with my two hands into the muddy shore and let my tears drip into the creek. It was like I had burst open some old, rotten, smouldering pus. I let it all drain out.

When I lifted my head, the shades of the setting sun were now quite different along the shoreline. How could the scene change in such a short time? Now there were shadows, and the shadows could become scary. I filled up the bucket at the clearest and deepest part of the creek and hurried back up the path to Grandma's place.

As I neared the cabin, I could hear laughter and quieter conversation. It was a very comforting sound. As I got into the light of the outside campfire, Grandma turned and said, "There's my Naens. The sunshine of my life. I don't know what I would do without her showing up once in awhile. That girl...reminds me of myself when I was that young.... Oh, Joshua, where does time go...eh?"

The old man's raspy response came. "No, Agnes, it is not where time went, it is where time is going."

Grandma giggled and nodded. "What I find scary is where it is going. I know where time went, because I was there, but I have no idea where time is going. I can only teach my granddaughter where we have been, in the hopes that she will know what to do with the time that is to come. But who truly knows what time is about?"

Joshua threw another log into the fire. "Old woman, it is times like this when you have to lower that moose nose I brought you into those smouldering embers and let it roast, while I fry up that fish."

I came up and deposited the pot beside the campfire. I felt much better and, for some reason, I felt much humility beside this old man. He reminded me of Hitz, but somehow, he seemed way beyond him...I could not explain. Maybe, if he was Hitz's father...yeah, I could accept that. The only problem was that this old man, Joshua, was no older than Hitz.

Anyway, I figure it amounts to what people can learn and see, and how they can understand what things are about in order to see more clearly. I had already noticed that there were very few people who could do that. From then on, I decided that Joshua would be my "Hitz" while I was here. I would listen and try to understand what he was saying. In that way, if I could not understand something, I could always ask Hitz, right?

Grandma already had the frying pan and her cooking stuff between them and I watched Joshua prepare the fish to fry. I saw that his hair was white all the way back from his temples when he removed his green cap and set it on the ground beside him. His face had no hair at all, except for his black eyebrows. The most striking thing about his face, though, was his eyes. They were so quick and alive, one glance would feel like he had been looking right straight at you. His hands looked large and strong, but they were also lean and long. As I studied his hands, his finger tapped the frying pan handle four times. I glanced up and found his twinkling, smiling eyes on me. I giggled and looked down. I was embarrassed that he'd caught me looking at him!

I jumped up because I knew he would need a plate for the fish. Once inside the cabin, I glanced around to see what else they would need. I decided to bring the salt and knife outside too. That gave me the chance to calm down so that I could pay closer attention.

Back beside the fire, I sat down and watched Grandma slicing up some of the meat Joshua had brought. As I sat across from them, I soon realized that their conversation sounded different when I was inside the cabin because I wasn't actually looking at them talking. Grandma and Joshua spoke only key words, and the silences I had noticed between the words were replaced with gestures of the hands; but more often it was the eyes and facial expressions that filled the silences.

While they made supper, I watched the movements that accompanied the conversation. Their words came quick, as did their actions, and most times I'd miss something. It was hard to read what was being said without actually staring at one of them, because then I'd miss the response from the other. At one point, their glances met and landed on me. Then Grandma glanced at the cabin and back to the cooked food. Plates! She wanted me to get the plates. I understood! I smiled and ran to the cabin for the plates. Grandma had a big smile on her face when I put the plates down beside the cooked food.

It was way on late when we finally finished our feast and went inside the cabin. Once inside, Joshua talked of times long gone and the teaching that went with every action that needed to be taken. This was a different form of speech. It was not a language of conversation. He sounded like he was talking to Grandma, but I soon realized it was me he was talking to! On and on he went, about every blade of grass and how the moose were very much akin to the humans in that they had their own system of doing things just as we did.

Then it hit me! He wanted to tell me something of the moose because I had really enjoyed my supper. I turned my head and looked at Joshua. He sat by the table, knees crossed, his hands clasped over one knee. I smiled and softly said, "Moose fed us tonight." A slow smile touched his face, accompanied by a slight nod of his head, and he said nothing more. After awhile, their conversation started again.

With a long yawn, I laid my head down on my cot as they continued talking under the coal oil lamp at the table. They talked about the pumps that would be driven into the ground so that we would have cleaner water; then they went outside. I heard Joshua saying, "Naens, come out here and see that bright moon. There's Chekabesh still holding his water pail!" What? I thought. What is he talking about, now? I swung my legs off the bed and went outside. Grandma was putting the pots away and banking up the cooking fire when I went outside and stood beside Joshua. There above the treetops was a giant, clear, round moon. I turned to him and smiled. Yeah, that was a nice moon all right.

He jerked his head, indicating the moon. "See that little boy there? He's still holding that pail in his hand? Well, that's Chekabesh. He was told never to look at the moon full in the face and certainly never to make fun of it. But that is exactly what Chekabesh did, and the moon swooped down because it was ticked off and swooped him up into the sky. And there he stands forever, holding his pail. That was to teach the kids to do as they were told or something would happen to them that could never be undone."

I looked at the moon. Yes, I had noticed that figure before, but the way my mother told it, it was a girl that was up there, but for the same reason – that she didn't listen when she was told not to look at the moon. I smiled up at Joshua. I would have to remember the name of Chekabesh, for I felt that wasn't the last time I would hear of him.

Just as quietly, Joshua walked away into the darkness.

I walked to the side of cabin and loaded my arms with wood. Out of habit, I knew that was what had to be done at the end of the day. When I came back inside, Grandma was already in bed and ready to blow out the lamp. I scampered to the bunk on the side of the room across from her and she blew out the light. The smell of the coal oil coil drifted up to me and I lay very quiet and still.

It was such an intense quiet that it took awhile for me to hear the dogs barking by the train station and way down the shoreline. Then I heard the voices of the people below the hill by the Anglican Church. Then all was still. The light and embers popped from the wood stove now and then, and I listened to Grandma's gentle breathing as she fell asleep. I lay awake for an awfully long time, wondering why this place affected me so differently than back home.

The next morning, I awoke to the sounds of birds singing. It smelled different too. I smelled only faint woodsmoke and fresh air. I listened some more to the birds in the quiet morning silence and then I heard a dog barking from way off, at the other end of the village. Then I heard someone splitting wood, somewhere to the east. Then the birds set up their chirping squabbles again. They made so much noise! Were they having a dispute or something? Just what was the problem?

When I heard Grandma stir, I asked, "Why are the birds yelling at each other? They sound like they're arguing about something."

Grandma swung her legs out of bed and sat looking at me as she stretched and yawned, then said in a quite puzzled voice, "Birds are arguing? That is not possible. What have they to argue about? Yes, they do let another group of birds know where their territory is, but they do not argue against each other. I think what you hear is something like, 'The sun is coming up! The sun is coming up! Let us all pray together to the Great Creator for giving us the voice to announce the beginning of another new day.'"

I pulled out my pillow and hit her squarely on the head! She giggled, and I laughed under my blankets as she got the fire going at the stove. Yeah, trust her to always come up with another view to my rather "narrow" one, as I was always finding out.

Grandma made coffee and bannock by the fireside outside as I got dressed in my "bush" clothes and came out. She had food laid out on the tablecloth. It looked like she was getting the food ready for packing. She looked at me and said, "You look like you, last summer, only a lot bigger. Didn't your mother send some jeans, pants, or something?"

I looked down at my overalls from last summer. They hung at least two inches above the ankles. No. It had never occurred to me that I would need different clothes. Since my summer clothes were here at Grandma's, I hadn't known that they would be too small now! Why hadn't Mama thought of that?

Grandma laughed. "Now, don't get all upset. We

could always let the hem down...but you see, your chest is now bigger and rather...just bursting out of your...overalls...top...." Then she went into such a giggling fit that she near doubled over the coffee pot that she was ready to put on the fire. What? What? Then she looked at me and her laughter died.

"Oh, don't look so stricken!" she said. "It's just so funny! If you only knew what your mother looked like in those things! Oh, my! She looked like a very shy, skinny, little boy who didn't even know how to go 'boo!' Now, here you are in the same overalls and you look like you are ready to say, 'Hey, You! All You Lousy, No-Good People of This Land, Hear What I Have To Say!!!'"

I stood and looked at her. I did not find that funny at all. What on earth was she talking about? Then she said, "Come here. Look!" I went to the fire and on the tablecloth were strips of the moose nose, ash-baked potatoes, some pemmican, canned corn, fried fish, wild carrot bunches, bannock, a jar of blueberry jam, and a pound of butter. I still didn't get it, until she said, "Which of those do you have in town and which do you have in the bush? When you put them all together, what you get is – you!"

I didn't say anything about that. I would have to think about it for awhile. I went back into the cabin and started packing up my "summer clothes," because I knew she would likely have someplace arranged for us to go. Sure enough, as soon as we had sampled a bit of this and that from the spread she had arranged by the campfire,

we were ready to go. The tent roll was outside, and I hauled the pots and pans to the canoe landing along with my bedroll and Grandma's, while she put the whole food box together.

As I loaded up the stuff into the canoe, I noticed that we had a lot less stuff than we usually did. What was going on? Were we coming back again soon? Or was our summer only for a week? I decided not to say anything and put my faith in Grandma to tell me what was going on. Maybe she didn't know right now. Was that why we only had a week's supply? That meant we would probably not even leave the lake.

We didn't. When we got clear of the last portage, Grandma suddenly steered the canoe to the right, toward the more cluttered islands leading to a narrow channel that eventually petered out to a little outward flowing steam. We got there in late evening. Grandma steered to the right and the front of the canoe went into a soft nudge of a very polite "hello" to the moss along the shoreline.

I got out and held the canoe while Grandma got out and made a bit of to-do about the landing and where we were going to set the tent. It appeared that she had the whole place set out and ready before my arrival, for there stood a set of brand new tent poles that someone had erected for her. There was even a surrounding of flat rocks to form the walls of a campfire. I began to get suspicious. Why would people do this?

We had no sooner set up camp and got the sheet of

pine branches on the floor when I heard the motorboat coming. I looked at Grandma. No! She shrugged and told me that there was a child, very overdue, and.... Now, I guessed, it was ready. I got my own meal together. The boat came and went and then I was all alone. Now I understood why we had brought so much cooked food. I had a slice of moose nose and a sip of tea. After that, I went to the bush behind the tent to have a pee, then put a big pile of wood on the campfire and went inside the tent. I lay for a long while, watching the fire pop and flicker against the canvas tent wall in the night until it began to fade.

I decided to get up one more time for the last cup of tea and to bank up the fire before I went to bed. Well, it didn't seem that there was any point in staying awake waiting for Grandma. So I banked up the fire, real high, and went inside the tent. I had on my comfy clothes, so that if I had to jump up and go somewhere, I could. I lay and listened and listened...but no sound came, save the popping of the fire, the frogs, the wind, the waves....

It was nearing six o'clock in the morning when I heard the motorboat come to drop Grandma off. The person didn't even stick around long enough for me to see who he was. There was Grandma coming up the path, very tired looking and very.... I couldn't put a word to it, like someone you could just envelop in your arms and all bad things would disappear! Well, there she was. There had been complications, and now mother and baby were on a way-freight train to the nearest hospital at Sioux

Lookout. Then, she had just been told this morning that someone else was sick and needed her immediate attention.

Nothing else was said of that as we paddled back to the community. Things did not go as they were supposed to that summer. I was ready to head home and tell Mama what had happened and that Grandma just was not in the mood for putting up with me this year. What was I to do? As we came up the path, Grandma slowed down and stood stock still. I walked up and stopped beside her.

"What's wrong, Grandma?"

She stared straight ahead, then whispered, "Someone has been in there." I rushed forward then, but she stayed where she was. I saw that the padlock had been pried off the door and was now just hanging loose. I slowly pushed the door and it swung open. I saw that things had been ransacked. Her cardboard storage boxes had been dumped on the floor, and the mattress was lying half off the bed, all her herb bags had been dumped on the floor, and the wooden food storage box had also been dumped.

I felt a strong rage sweep over me! I ran inside and grabbed the stuff off the floor. I started yelling, "What the heck were they looking for? What did they think they'd find? Why didn't they just look into the things to see if they could find what they were looking for? Why did they have to do this! Who would do this?"

Suddenly, Grandma was there in front of me. She closed her arms around me and held me there, all while whispering, "They are gone. They were here, now they are gone. Whatever they took, they thought they needed. They are here no more."

I gasped in exasperation. "I can see that they're not here anymore! What would they hang around for? They would steal from an old woman and they should still be here?"

Her arms were around me tighter still, she whispered, "No, I mean they are not here in spirit any longer. Their spirits have gone elsewhere long ago. They don't care what they do here."

I lifted my head. "What do you mean, their spirits are gone...do you mean their spirits have gone to the devil already and it doesn't matter what they do now?"

She paused. "Hmm, if you put it that way, that could also be true. But what I meant was that they did something bad and they did it knowing that it was a bad thing to do, so what is there to do anything about now? It has been done. What I am left with now, is knowing that all the money I had saved up for the last five years was hidden in my dry Labrador tea bag dumped in the corner of the table over there."

My glance fell on the bag and I felt sick. She had been saving money to get me out here for the Christmas holidays. I felt the tears streaming down my face, but I made no noise.

I DID NOT GO HOME, but stayed with Grandma at the cabin for the rest of the summer. Grandma introduced me to the village and all its people. She took me on a tour around the whole community one day. We started off on the path along the lake and came back around through the path on the other side of the railroad tracks. My first near mistake was my impulse to introduce myself to the occupants of the first cabin we came across, but Grandma caught my eye before I made a fool of myself. When we left the cabin, I walked slowly behind Grandma and tugged her sweater.

"That was me – the butter right out of the store refrigerator!" I had finally figured out what she'd meant about the food she'd spread out on the tablecloth that time. She laughed, but didn't say anything. The second time was when Grandma stopped at another door and I was about to knock, but she pulled my arm back in time. I smiled at her and whispered, "That was me – the can of corn." This time, she had to stop her giggle when the door opened for us to come in.

I came to know and understand that the meaning of an extended family also stretched to include the whole community. The person I often heard chopping wood in the mornings turned out to be the bachelor across the railroad tracks who went around splitting wood for old people. And when something happened or needed to be done, everyone pitched in to help. Like the guy in the motorboat who came and got Grandma from our campsite happened to live next door to the family of the woman who was having the baby. In this way, I finally understood why Grandma immediately dropped what she was doing to go where she was needed.

One morning, when Grandma came in from the outhouse, she set down a piece of folded brown paper on the table and said nothing at all. I got up, quite curious, wondering what it was, since she was not saying anything at all about it. As she was getting the fire started, I reached for the paper. It looked like the inner brown paper of a sugar bag. I unfolded it and there lay some money. I counted six twenties, five tens and six fives. I set the paper down and looked at her, totally puzzled. She said nothing as she proceeded to fill the teapot.

In jest, I suddenly grabbed the money, flipped the stove lid open, and held it over the open fire, saying, "Well? Does it exist, or shall I just drop it and pretend we never saw the money?"

She took her time reaching the stove, where she flipped the lid back down and set the teapot on top. Then she reached for the money and put it on the table. I sat down and waited. Finally, she sighed and said, "It is very sad, really. I imagine that whoever saw fit to return some of my money found out who had stolen it and most assuredly has gone to great hardship to come up with that amount. As you know, no one has that kind of money just lying about."

I was surprised that someone would do such a thing if they didn't steal it in the first place. "You think maybe they took up a collection?" She paused, but did not say anything. I thought about that as I washed my face and said nothing more about it, because I had also realized that Grandma would have no idea who left the money by the door. I saw her tuck the money back into her dry Labrador tea bag and shove it under her mattress.

I smiled. "Chitamoo, make sure you hide your nuts right back in the same place they were stolen from." She made a face at me.

"So, who are you now?" she asked.

"Pemmican," I replied.

THE BICYCLE

SEPTEMBER BEGAN WITH GREAT EXCITEMENT AT THE upcoming wedding, which was set for the middle of October. I had begged Grandma to come and so had Mama, but there was no way she could. It appeared that my Aunt Vera needed her at that time because she was expecting a baby. I was really disappointed with that, because I had wanted Grandma with me very badly.

After school, sometime in the middle of September, I lagged behind Cindy and the boys on the way home. I was actually more like dragging my feet. Mama had mailed out a long list of invitations and there hadn't been much of a response. I knew Mama was worried. She had wanted her mother and sisters with her, but that was not to be, except that maybe Aunt Martha would come. I did not particularly like Aunt Martha. She was Mama's older sister and tended to be quite bossy. I liked my Aunt Vera better, but she couldn't come either. I thought, though, that Mama was afraid of meeting Dave's family. Dave said they were rich city Native people. What if they didn't like us?

A noise caught my attention and when I lifted my head, lo and behold, there was Hitz, coming toward me, wobbling and swerving...on a bicycle! He came on, knees stuck out to the sides, churning and pumping up and down. The tip of his old toque bobbed to the left and right as he descended on me, faster and faster. His elbows shot out as he hit a bump on the road and his knees continued to pump periodically as he came on, swerving to the left and right!

I held my breath as he spurted toward me, wavering and teetering. I got ready to jump to the left or right. He was totally focussed on the bicycle, and just as he put his head up to see me, the bike took a dive into the ditch. He pitched forward and flew, face first, into the dirt and managed to shovel quite a bit of mud over his face before he came to a skidding halt!

By this time, I was near to busting with laughter, but I waited to see if he was all right. He sat bolt upright, took a swipe of the mud off the side of his face, and knocked off the chunk of dry grass hanging from his ear. Then he turned his bewhiskered face toward me and produced a gaping hole of a grin.

I still had not moved from where I stood, but suddenly a strong welling sensation built up within me, and for the first time that I could remember, my whole body went into a huge spasm of laughter. This was even worse than the Christmas play. My voice sounded very, very strange in my ears as I burst into uncontrolled laughter! I laughed and laughed, until he came up in his whole muddy-covered body and stopped in front of me.

Then a very strange thing happened. My laughter suddenly turned into tears, and there I was, bawling my eyes out. I cried and cried like the whole inside of me had burst a dam. Then I felt his arms close around me and he held me tight until I got myself under control again.

After a whole five minutes or so, I was able to look up at him again, and this time my giggles turned into laughter again, because he still had mud clinging to the sides of his head, like he had decided to dig part of the culvert up with his head! He, too, started to laugh and that got me going even more, because he sounded like an old cow that tried to hiccup and just ended up grunting instead! And then his heaving and rasping took on the sound of a squealing pig!

By then I was laughing so hard that I bent down with my hands on my shaking knees, and stood up again just as he apparently was about to bend over me – and I whacked him on the chin with the top of my head. I heard a squishing, crunching sound as he howled in pain and did a fancy spin-around jig that got some of the mud flying off his clothes.

I looked up at him when he stopped and then, on impulse, I gave him a peck on the cheek. When I stepped back, for some reason, that little action had brought a wave of emotion over him that sent tears brimming in his eyes! Now what had I done? I did not know what to do! It was then that I realized he had pasted mud all over me too! My mouth fell open as I looked at the mud down the front of my coat and over my shoulders. Hitz just hunched up his ragged shoulders and nodded at his mud-encrusted bike.

"H'it's old. Found it in the dump. Took a ride. See if I can fix it."

I smiled and nodded. "It looks good. I don't know much about bikes, but I think if you take it to Jake at the gas station, he could fill the tires and make sure it works okay."

He smiled at me. "Oh, yes. Jake. H'it's a good idea. Thank you, Ray. I will take it to Jake."

I nodded and walked by him. As always, I looked back. I saw him pull the bike out and push it along the road, and then he gave a little hop and a skip as he always did, as if he knew I was watching him. I smiled and walked on home.

A few weeks later, Mama called me from my bedroom where I was trying to do my homework. I slammed the book shut and went into the kitchen and there stood Hitz! Mama was by the stove, and with a smile she nodded at Hitz and he in turn nodded at her with a smile before he directed his attention at me. I wondered what he was up to. I followed him out the door and down the driveway and there...was a red bicycle! I looked at Hitz. Was this a new bike of his? Was he here to show me that he'd finally got a brand new bike? But he didn't look back at me as his baggy pants flapped from side to side as he walked to the bike. When I came to a stop beside him, he pulled the bicycle up and pushed it toward me.

"H'it's not new. Found it at the dump. Got the guy at the gas station to fix it up and it not cost anything at all.... No need to pay me...so there you are. H'its your bike. I knew it was for you the minute I saw it!"

Still not understanding, I stood there looking at him. Did he say it was mine? How could it be mine? I didn't even know how to ride one! I'd never even thought of owning such a thing! I looked at Hitz, shaking my head.

"I can't take it, Hitz. I didn't pay for it and there's no way I could save enough money to pay for it.... So I can't take it!"

He leaned on the bike, patting it. "H'well, you see, this poor fella got thrown into the dump because some-body not want him anymore. You can see, nothing wrong with him, and I even check with Jake at the gas station. We changed the tires and filled them with air, and now, this guy he is so happy that somebody going to ride him and take care of him and change his tires when he need them, but most of all, he needs someone to use him and take care of him. I thought you would be the perfect person for him."

I realized this was the longest speech Hitz had ever spoken in all the years I had known him! I looked at the bike. It was a red bike. I could make it into a shiny red bike. I could learn to ride it and it could take me to many places I would rather not walk to...and it would be...mine! I smiled. Yes, Hitz was right. The bike needed me as much as I needed it!

I looked down at the bike. "But Hitz, I don't know how to ride a bike! I don't know anything about bikes!"

Suddenly, his face cracked into a toothless grin. "Come, I show you!"

With Hitz behind me, I pedalled as he pushed the bike, until I finally figured out the balance as I rode to the end of the road. I didn't know the precise moment he let go and suddenly I was on my own! I reached the end of the road, then turned around and headed back toward the house. I watched him weave to the left and right, in time to the swaying of the bike, until I came to a stop in front of him. He waved his hands, gesturing in a perfect imitation of the day he crashed his face into the mud. I got off the bike, laughing at the memory, when he suddenly grabbed me and spun me around like a little kid! That was when I saw Mama at the window.

She disappeared from the window and then she was at the door, walking very quickly toward us. I stood beside Hitz and the bike, waiting. She came to a halt in front of us, stuck her face close to the old man, and spoke in a very stern voice. "You are not to touch my daughter as if she was a little kid, understand? So how much do I owe you for this...bike?"

Hitz stopped as though struck across the face and

remained silent for a full minute before he lowered his head and said, almost in a whisper, "No. You not owe me anything, madam. I not pay anything for the bike. She my friend and...she is...like daughter to me. I would never let harm come to her...I not mean to be disrespectful. Please, you will let her keep it?"

Mother heaved a big sigh and stepped back. Nodding at Hitz, she said, "Since I let you bring it to her, I did allow you to give it to her. Now, I still want to give you something for it, so that I don't feel like I owe you something. Do you understand?"

Hitz nodded and, with this bit of encouragement, I thought of something. I said, "Wait, Hitz." I ran inside the house and into my bedroom. After some rummaging around in my closet, I came up with my father's old beaver-skin hat! I ran out and Mama was nowhere in sight, but Hitz still remained slowly shuffling his feet beside the bike.

I ran up and yanked off his old toque and...he had no hair under there! He must have noticed my look of surprise, for his mouth opened into a gaping hole of a grin as I plunked the beaver-skin hat down over his head. To my dismay, his eyes disappeared underneath the fur! It was too big. He nodded his head, and now I was looking at a big nodding beaver-skin hat with a big gaping mouth underneath it!

By this time, my giggles were turning into outright laughter as the beaver-skin hat continued to bob on top of his bald head. I whipped the hat off his head, shoved the toque inside it, and crammed it back down on his head. Now his eyes twinkled in merriment from under the beaver fur.

I stepped back and, trying to keep a straight face, I said softly, "That looks nice, Hitz. That was my father's beaver-skin hat."

He nodded, and the hat stayed in place. "Yeah, you wear it in winter sometime. I wear it all the time. I take good care of it. Thank you, Ray." He sidestepped around me and marched very smartly down the road with his newly acquired beaver-skin hat sitting firmly on his head. I turned and noticed my mother by the window, holding her hand over her mouth and shaking her head.

I practised getting on the bike and trying to keep it upright, but it kept falling to the side. Mama was busy making supper, so I was on my own. I'd get on and then would have to hop off as soon as it started to tip over if I didn't want my face shovelling dirt into my mouth.

Luckily, Dave arrived with the boys. The truck had no sooner stopped than the boys descended on me! I hadn't thought of them at all! I should have known! The bike was swiped away from me and was going down the road between the three boys before I could say a thing. Then Dave came to my rescue and the bike was put back into my hands amidst howls of protest. From then on, I allowed the boys to keep the bike upright until I could ride it by myself. In return, I would teach them how to ride the bike, only because then Mama could send them to the store to get some milk or something when Dave was not home, so I wouldn't have to go. Either way, my bike would come in handy.

On Saturday morning, everyone was still sound asleep when I got up. So I figured I would ride down the road to the west and see if I could find Hitz's home. I knew we had gone down there sometimes when Charlie used to pick him up to go into town. Now, here I was ready for my first bike ride. I softly knocked on Mother's door to let her know where I was going. To my surprise, she was standing by the window. I whispered, "I'm going for a ride on the bike."

She answered, "Don't go too far. I'll be making breakfast soon and...be careful on that thing." I nodded and closed the door again.

I left the house and headed west down the road. Soon another gravel road branched out to the northwest and I kept going. There were no houses this far from town and the gravel road was pretty rough. Early morning mist still hung heavy and frosty along the bushes on both sides of the road. Over a sharp outcrop of rocks beside the road, I noticed a lake between the trees. I remembered this now. I was getting close to Hitz's place!

After what seemed like too long a time, just as I was beginning to worry that I had made a wrong turn after all, I saw the fallen-down sign on the side of a hill. As the bike took the turn, I let the wheels run and rested while the bike slid down the hill, and off to the right, I could see the lake again. Then I saw the turnoff to Hitz's place! That was where he used to stand waiting for us!

I stopped at the turnoff and wondered which of the cabins by the lake was his. I sat resting and breathing hard, when out from under a bushy driveway, came Hitz on his own bike! His beaver-skin hat remained firmly in place as he bumped over a couple of potholes. His face broke into a bewhiskered grin when he saw me.

He came to a stop beside me and I asked, "How did you make the hat fit?"

He pulled it off and showed me how he had sewn his old toque to the beaver-skin hat along the edges, so that the hat now fit snugly over his toque. I burst out laughing and he shoved it back on his bald head. A look of concern crossed his face.

"What you doing here, Ray? Your mama, she gonna be real mad. You come too far. Come, I take you back."

Before I could say anything, he was off puffing and ped-alling up the hill. I followed and gained on him. By the time we came up over the hill, it had become a race. With my hair flying over my shoulders, I glanced back to see that Hitz had hunkered down over the handlebars, with the wind flattening down the fur of his beaver hat. He would come up, gaining on me, and then I would pull away again.

I glanced back again and saw that he was making ges-tures, and I kept looking at him trying to figure out what he was trying to say. I slowed just in time to avoid the grinding rush of air as big tires spun and screeched, spraying sand and gravel over me! I'd never even seen the truck pulling out from a side road!

Hitz came to a skidding stop beside me as the driver leaned out and yelled back at me to be more careful. The truck took off as I sat there shaking and Hitz was wheezing, with spit flying all over the place.

"Sheesh! Sheesh! Dang it, girl, why wasn't you watching! Eh, eh, this not good. Your mama, she gonna hit me for this. No, she gonna kill me for this! I know it, she gonna kill me!"

I felt my face break into a grin, and then he caught my eye and we started laughing again. Oh, that was so funny! You should have seen Hitz's face! Oh, he looked like a peeled-back weasel with a big bushy head! He started his bike again, slower this time, and I followed him right to the first turn leading to our street. He let me ride on and I waved back. He was still sitting there looking at me.

Hitz never allowed me to go down the road toward his place again. We went riding together, though, to the town dump where he had picked up the bikes. I had never known such a place existed. Hitz also made me promise that I would never come down this road in the summer, as there would be wild bears prowling around looking for food. He didn't need to say anything further. I was afraid of wild animals because I did not know them.

Though I had never seen a real live bear, Hitz said they

were very dangerous. If one saw me alone on the bike, it would chase me and knock me off the bike and eat me! He said they ran so fast, I would never be able to go fast enough on the bike to get away from one. In all the time I had spent with Grandma, we had never seen a bear. I would remember to ask her about bears the next time I saw her.

One evening, Mama and I sat at the kitchen table going over the list of people who were coming to the wedding. There would be Mama's sister Martha and her husband Joe, Dave's older brother Jeff and his wife Mary, Dave's younger brother John and his wife Maggie, and Dave's parents, James and Marion. I started giggling and then Mother burst into laughter. What was with the "J's" and "M's?"

Mama had never met any of Dave's family, since they all lived in Toronto. Oh, the thought of city people staying in our little cabin! There was one hotel downtown, but it was all rundown, dirty, and a place where the drunks hung out. So Dave and Mama had decided to invite everyone to our house.

We were curious about Dave's family. Even his sons didn't know them very well. It seemed that the only time Dave and his sons visited them was during the summer holidays. They had never been to visit here, because they didn't like to leave the city to come to a little "mill town" like ours.

The next question was where they were all supposed to sleep. Thank goodness no one was bringing children, so the boys' bedroom with the two beds would be given over for Jeff and Mary and Martha and Joe. Cindy and I would keep our own room, but my bed would be hauled over to Mama's room. So Mama's bigger bedroom with its now two beds would be occupied by John and Maggie and James and Marion. The boys were to cram into Dave's bedroom and that left Mama and Dave. Where were they to sleep? Mama decided that they would bunk out in the living room.

When Dave came home that evening, he saw the list of guests and their sleeping quarters and burst out laughing. It appeared that there would be a problem with the occupants in Mama's bedroom, since Maggie and James did not get along so well. So it was decided that all the women would occupy Mama's room and all the men would occupy the boys' bedroom. The couch in the corner of the living room would be pulled out into a bed for Dave and Mama, since they were going to get up early to make breakfast for everyone anyway.

With that settled, we moved on to the issue of what to cook and how the meals were to be dished out. It was exhausting work, but I spent a lot of time with Mama, since I was helping her with the planning and running around town looking for ribbons, flowers, bows, and things she would need to decorate the little cabin. A trip to the second-hand shop supplied extra towels and sheets that we needed, which required several days of washing before the sheets were ready to spread out on the beds. The boys were moved into their new quarters by the first week of October.

THE WEDDING

O N FRIDAY MORNING, WE ALL GOT UP EARLY AND prepared the little cabin for our guests. The weather outside, however, was not cooperating. It was very windy and the sleet had turned to big flakes of snow. Dave had taken the day off to arrange for his own worries. He needed a haircut and the suit he was to wear would have to be picked up from where he had taken it for alterations.

Mama's dress was ready and hanging in her room. It was a very soft, pink, flowing dress with ribbons and little flowers along the collar line. The delicate pink and white flowers to be pinned on her hair were ready. Her matching pink shoes were also tucked neatly beneath the dress. Dave had insisted she not cut her hair, because he loved it long and flowing as it was right now. So Delores, the hairdresser, was coming to our cabin early Saturday morning to arrange Mama's hair.

The wedding was to take place Saturday at two in the

afternoon, and the reception would follow at the church hall at the back of the church. After that, everyone would come back here to the cabin. Our guests were expected to start arriving this afternoon or evening. Martha and Joe would be arriving on the afternoon train at four o'clock, and Dave would be there to pick them up. The Toronto people would have arrived by plane at Fort William this morning. Since there were six of them, they would rent two cars at Fort William and then drive to get here around four o'clock in the afternoon.

I was standing at the stove with Mama when she caught my eye and I turned to the boys at the table. My mouth flew open when I saw the hair on the back of Henry's neck. It was cut very high and crooked. He was almost bald an inch from the base of his hairline. Mother said in a low voice in Ojibwa, "Todd apparently noticed it was a little crooked and tried to fix it."

I said, "But it's still crooked."

She smiled. "He probably would have kept on going until he got to the top of little brother's head if Dave hadn't walked into their bedroom."

I giggled as I turned the eggs over. I liked our quiet private talks and comments. Grandma had greatly improved my Ojibwa language and the quiet chats with Mama kept the words from fading in my memory. There was an unspoken understanding between us that we never spoke our language when Dave or the boys were around.

Dave did not know the language and apparently neither did any of his family. The way I understood it, Dave's parents were raised in the city and both had been adopted by non-Native people. They had grown up never knowing their Native heritage. When they met and got married, they had the three sons, but Dave was the only one who identified himself as a Native. By birth, his mother was Ojibwa and his father was Mohawk.

When the boys were around eight, ten, and twelve years old, their father had died. Then they got a stepfather. He was a well-known businessman in Toronto. His family had come from England, and I understood that he had been a Shakespearean actor in his younger days. He would be a very interesting man, I thought.

By the time we cleaned up the morning meal, Dave went off in the truck with the boys and Mama and I did some last minute shuffling between the packed freezer in the corner of the porch and the stuff in the fridge. As the snow deepened outside, I went out and swept the doorstep and the back step toward the outhouse. We did not have an indoor bathroom, so the path to the outhouse also had to be shovelled in the winter. There were two holes on the wide bench-like seat inside the outhouse. One hole was larger than the other.

Mama had laughed so hard she was near to tears when she came back from the outhouse yesterday. Dave, in a last-minute stroke of genius, had nailed on two toilet seats with lids and the seat on the smaller hole was now covered with pink fluffy material. There were stacks of toilet paper on each side of the bench, with a couple of magazines beneath. There was a small window on each side and the door sported a shiny new latch inside.

As I came around the corner of the cabin, the truck had just pulled up and the boys piled out with shouts of excitement. I followed them inside and there they stood, each holding a suit against them. Mama smiled. "You will look like nice little gentlemen, but will you behave as gentlemen?"

They all responded, "Yeah, sure we will!" Cindy was at the table eating cookies and she giggled at the boys. Her dress was the first to be made back in the summer, and Mama had finished mine when I returned from Grandma's in September.

All too soon, Dave had to rush off to the train station. We waited anxiously, hoping that Dave's people would not show up while he was gone. The train was on time, and in less than half an hour, the truck returned and Martha and Joe came through the door. Aunt Martha was a big woman, tall and broad. Her hair was bushy and curly, and she seemed to sport a permanent scowl across her face. Joe, on the other hand, was short and very skinny and liked to laugh a lot.

After introductions to the boys, she turned to me and said, "My, my, look at the size of that girl! Even her eyes look greener than they used to be. How old are you now, girl?"

I smiled and answered, "Twelve."

But she'd already turned to Mama, exclaiming, "Kate,

how do you manage with five children, and three of them boys?"

I stood still, looking at Mama. She was Kate. I had never thought of her as "Kate." Her name was Kathryn, but everyone called her Kate. Tomorrow David and Kathryn would be married, and what about me?

For some reason, I was beginning to feel like I might not fit in with this new family. The boys and little Cindy were all right. But where did I belong? I was older and I was a girl. I was afraid that I would become more Kate's live-in helper. I wished Grandma was here!

I turned and grabbed my coat and went outside. I went to the boys' rubber tube, still hanging on a rope under the tree, and sat down. I was swaying back and forth when I noticed a car drive by slowly, followed by another. I didn't usually see those around...wait! They must be Dave's family! I ran to the back door, flung the door open, and yelled, "Dave! Dave! They're here! They're here!"

I hovered around the woodpile and saw Dave pulling on his coat as he made his way down the driveway to the road. I saw him waving and then he waited awhile before the cars came back and pulled in behind the truck. Dave helped the woman out of the first car. Her white hair curled out from under her little black hat. The man also had white hair with a hat on top, and he was tall, almost as tall as Dave. I watched them shake hands and then the occupants of the other car got out. All four of them. Dave's two brothers and their wives.

The ladies had been in the back seat and were now stumbling around the car in...small black city shoes. The old woman also had high heels on her little boots with their little fur-trimmed tops. The men wore long coats. Man, did they ever look strange! I hurried in through the back door. I wanted to see them coming through the front door with big Aunty Martha sitting there waiting for the door to open!

Dave came in first, followed by his father and mother. Behind them were the two men and then two women. Martha nodded to each in turn as Dave made the introductions, but she did not get up. Kate was by the door and greeted each one with a handshake as Dave introduced them. Soon they were all in the living room, and Kate disappeared into our bedroom where she dumped their coats. I stood by the stove and waited for Kate to come and get me to help her with the coffee and cakes she had all set out on the kitchen table. Martha and Joe had been filling their faces since they arrived.

Kate came in and gestured for me to pick up the tray of cakes. I was introduced as soon as the boys had finished lining up for the greetings. When they had all taken a seat in the living room, I passed the tray around and each one took a cake and a coffee cup. But before Dave's mother took anything, she wanted to be shown where the bathroom was. Kate glanced at Dave.

Dave leaned toward his mother. "Mom, I told you we have an outhouse."

To which the old lady answered, "Why, yes, dear. You said there was an outhouse. By that I understood you to mean an outside cottage or guest cabin?"

Dave patted her arm and smiled. "No, Mom. An outhouse is like an outdoor biffy, you understand? We do not have an indoor bathroom."

The old woman drew in her breath and glanced at her husband. The old gentleman sat there smiling and said to her, "Well, dear. Off you go. Put your coat and boots back on and...off you go to the outhouse."

She gave a big huff at his teasing and Kate nudged me. I offered, "I will show you the way, ma'am."

Kate had gone to fetch her coat and I went to the back door and slipped my jacket and boots on. The old woman walked across the kitchen, her heels click-clicking across the floor, and I saw the glance that passed from Kate to Martha, with a warning not to open her mouth, or else! I smiled and went out the back door with madam behind me. She stopped as she stepped outside and stood there taking in a big breath. I stopped and waited.

Then she said, "The air is so fresh here. Very fresh, and I can actually smell the scent of the pine trees. Oh, it is indeed lovely. Look at all the trees. What is beyond the treeline back there...Ray, was it?"

I nodded my head as she caught up to me. "Well, there are no more houses back there, just trees and more trees, and where the train tracks turn, then you cross the railroad tracks and into more and more trees." As I continued toward the outhouse, I could hear her trudging along behind me. When we got there, I stepped aside and pulled the outhouse door open for her. She had crossed her hands over her waist and stood there looking at the wooden bench with the two toilet seats.

I smiled. "The pink one, Dave made that for you yesterday." I don't know what made me say that, but I could just tell that if anyone could appreciate such a thing, she would. She smiled at me and entered. I closed the door and walked a ways down the path, when I heard muffled laughter coming from the outhouse. I giggled and waited. I could see where the heels of her little boots had sunk deep into the mud and snow. When she came out, I commented, "Kate has many pairs of winter boots. Your boots look like the same size and she wouldn't mind you borrowing a pair to wear around the place."

"Oh. Then I will ask her. My, you have such wonderful green eyes," she said as I stepped aside to let her walk ahead. I found that very strange. That was the first time a stranger had looked at me without thinking my green eyes were odd on my face. I could usually tell what they were thinking. I was happy that she thought my eyes looked wonderful! I liked her.

"Call me Gram Marion, that's what all my grandchildren call me," she continued as she walked slowly and carefully back to the cabin.

"How many grandchildren do you have?" I asked.

"Well now, at last count...I have twelve all together,

that's including all five of you here." It surprised me that she already considered us as her grandchildren. Quite pleased, I said nothing more. When we entered through the back door, she exclaimed as she stepped in, "Oh, what a lovely bathroom. Fluffy pink seat and all!"

Martha set up a howling laugh from the kitchen table. "Yeah," she said, " I near peed my pants laughing when I saw that!"

Joe nudged at her and whispered in Ojibwa, "Watch your language now!"

Martha pushed her elbow at him, saying in English, "Oh, you! Ain't said nothing un-proper!"

My attention turned to Kate as she knelt down and pulled the old lady's boots off where she sat leaning back on the couch. I smiled as Kate walked by me, saw her glance at the muddy, grass-encrusted pointy heels. She came back with one of her own more sturdy new low-heeled boots that she had planned to wear on her wedding day and knelt down in front of the old lady again and tugged the boots on.

After examining her feet, the old lady smiled and said she would be very thankful to wear them while she was here with us. The other two women leaned forward and made faces at each other, meaning that they wouldn't be caught dead wearing such things! I glanced at Dave sitting on a chair by the door and noticed that he was watching me. His face broke into a big smile, and I knew exactly what he was thinking. The entrance of the church hall was all mud at this time of year. Now, with the ground newly covered with deep snow, the ladies would sink up to the tops of their tiny high-heeled boots if the mud did not freeze solid tonight.

After the tea and cakes, everyone got up and hurried back and forth getting their suitcases unpacked in their rooms. Since Martha had already unpacked and claimed one of the beds, she was there to help Kate with the supper. The boys went outside to play around by the woodpile at the back of the cabin. Cindy was alone in our bedroom, sitting on the chair by the window, looking out at the boys. I approached and swept her hair off her forehead and tucked it behind her ears. "What's the matter, Cindy?"

She looked up at me. "You didn't hear? Martha is not sleeping with those ladies, so she's taking our bed and we have to sleep on the floor. I don't want to sleep on the floor and I don't like Aunty Martha in our room!"

I sat down and whispered, "Don't say that too loud, it will make Mama sad. Aunty Martha is her sister, remember? That would be like a little girl telling you she didn't want me in her room. How would you feel then?" She put her head down and nodded. Then I said, "Come, it will be like camping outside. Remember, we used to make a tent up on the hill at our old house?"

Her face lit up and we attacked the closet. We brought forth a mosquito netting that Mama used outside sometimes. We strung that right over our makeshift mattress and bedding on the floor. Cindy was laughing and giggling as she dove into the blankets.

The evening meal was another adventure. All the food was set out on the table and the paper plates came in handy when the clean dishes ran out, and still they had not finished. There were fifteen people eating, after all. When the roast, potatoes, gravy, and vegetables were finished, pots of tea and coffee were set to brew and I helped the ladies washing and drying the dishes. When that was done, the cakes and pies soon filled the table. The process repeated itself again with the dishes and paper plates and cups.

Finally, the meal was over and it was very dark outside. The radio played in the living room and they all sat around talking and laughing at days gone by or at things Dave had done that we hadn't heard about. Kate stayed with Dave in the living room and I helped Aunt Martha and Mary with the cleaning up. Maggie was not the sort for kitchen stuff. Mary said that Maggie had a maid to do all the cleaning and cooking for her as well as to look after her four children.

Aunt Martha turned from the tub of hot dishwater, wiping her hands on the dish towel. "Then, what does she do all day? Sit around on her butt?"

Mary put a finger to her lips, reminding Martha not to speak so loudly. Mary had bright red polish on her long fingernails and she was carefully trying to wipe a cup dry. My glance caught Martha's and I could tell she was thinking the same thing. It would be mighty difficult to do any housekeeping with those fingernails. I could not imagine someone not doing anything at all in their own home, for their own children, or even for themselves. How sad, I thought.

Aunt Martha had come to the same conclusion, for she was now telling Mary about all the hard work Mama had to do and how she, Aunt Martha, took great pride in looking after her own children too. She told Mary about all the hours Mama had spent at the sewing machine to make her own wedding dress and our clothes as well. Mary pursed her lips and shook her head, sadly.

I decided to go outside for fresh air. I was heading for the rubber tube at the tree when I noticed someone sitting in it. "Billy?" There was no response. I walked closer and took the rope in my hand beside his. "Billy? What are you doing here?"

He shrugged. "Nothing."

"What's the matter, Billy?"

"Nothing."

I stood a moment longer before I figured out what to say. "Billy. I'm your sister. Whatever happened to us in the past, we have been through it together. It's something we can talk about. Now, pretend I'm "Nothing." Tell Nothing what the problem is. Nothing will hear, and maybe Nothing can help."

He gave a big sigh. "Okay, Nothing. They all remembered Todd and Henry, but they didn't know what to say to me...made me feel like I didn't belong. Maybe never will!"

I gave the rope a slight push that set him swaying.

"They had never seen you before, how are they supposed to know anything about you? What would Grandma say to Todd and Henry? She's never met them either."

Billy's question came quickly. "What would Grandma say to Henry if she saw him for the first time tonight?"

Grandma's words came immediately to mind and I did a good imitation of her. "Tilt your head to the side a bit, boy, to even your hair out before it gets seasick!"

Billy burst out laughing and I stood there smiling. The sound of his laughter was so much like our father's. But Billy would never remember that.

We went back into the house and Billy joined the other boys in the back room. I picked up the dishcloth in the kitchen again and listened to the information exchange between Mary and Aunt Martha. Mary's own three children were grown up, like Martha's. I understood that Maggie was about the same age as my Aunt Vera and that she had four little ones.

I listened as I put stuff away and replaced the cups, plates, and utensils on the shelf. Gram Marion never even entered the kitchen, but sat on the couch, propped up with several pillows that Jeff had pulled from the bedrooms. I wondered who was going to be yelling later about not having a pillow!

When Dave came in to chat with Mary, Aunt Martha nudged him with her elbow and asked, "What you doing here then, if you got such a rich family in Toronto?"

Dave turned and smiled at Aunt Martha. "Well, I

decided that after graduation...."

Mary cut in. "Him and his university degree, and here he is in this godforsaken place!"

Dave responded, "Mary, it is not a godforsaken place! It's a wonderful place where people like Kate and...Ray, here, live. You'll meet most of our friends tomorrow and they're real down-to-earth Native people...like Charlie! You've got to meet Charlie, you will never meet a nicer man! Just how many Native people do you have as friends, Mary? Or, do you even know anything about Native people?" Mary's eyes widened. She glanced around, but did not respond.

With Aunt Martha's question forgotten now, we listened to Mary and Dave talking about the good and bad points of living in a city as opposed to living in a small town like ours. Joe had remained seated at the kitchen table, where he had been since he first arrived. When Dave left the room, he kept Mary entertained with his many stories of life in the bush-cutting business. Mary seemed sincerely interested in the lifestyle here in a small northwestern town.

After another round of tea and coffee, everyone began yawning, and I was surprised to see that the clock was nearing eleven and the boys had already crawled into bed. I went into our bedroom to find Cindy fast asleep inside the mosquito netting. I kicked off my shoes, pulled off my dress, and snuggled into bed with my slip on. I had no idea where my nightgown had gone during the day's quick reshuffle to accommodate Aunt Martha.

When I awoke the next morning, there was Joe's gaping snoring mouth on my bed beside my Aunt Martha! He was not supposed to sleep in here! I scrambled up and quickly changed into clean clothes for the day. I would put on my dress for the wedding later on.

I slowly opened the door and went into the kitchen to find Dave and Kate already there at the table sipping coffee. I picked up a cup, poured myself some coffee, and sat down directly across from them. I said, "My dear Lady Madam and Sir Knight. May I take this pleasure...." Dave whipped a dishtowel off the table and draped it over my head.

I rolled the edge up and peered from underneath, whispering, "Why, my dear Lord. How have I offended thee?" I noticed that Kate was looking behind me with an amused smile on her face. I pulled the towel off my head and turned around. It was Grampa James, as everyone called him. He stood there a second before he stepped forward and bowed to Dave.

"Have I interrupted something, M'Lord? Should I alert Mistress Marion that a knave has arrived with a message, perhaps?"

"Not a knave, Sir James," Dave replied. "Why, it is the Lady Ray, Sir. Her brave Knight in Shining Armour has escorted her to this castle to inform us that today is the day." Dave glanced at Kate, who was now doing her best to suppress her laughter. "It has been granted by his Royal Highness that today is the day that I shall wed my dear Lady Kate."

Sir James turned to me. "Pray tell, Lady Ray, who is this Knight in Shining Armour who protects you so well?"

At this point, when Kate started sputtering into her hand and before I could say anything, Dave replied in surprised shock. "Why, Sir James! Have you never heard of the gallant knight, Hitz?"

Mama burst out laughing. "Oh my! Now I know where Dave got this castle stuff!"

Gram Marion came around the corner just then and flipped her hand at Grampa James. "Oh, he's on that old castle stuff again. They used to absolutely destroy my living room with their sword fights. All four of them, Sir James and his Three Musketeers. Good heavens, the mess, not to mention the noise!" Somehow, no one had mentioned that last night. They had gone on and on about childhood escapades and how each of them became successful businessmen...except for Dave, perhaps, though no one said it in so many words. I remembered Dave in his hunter's clothing, carrying his rifle and hunting knife, and I could not imagine that these men were really his brothers and that the big old Englishman with the neatly trimmed hair was his stepfather.

After another gigantic effort at making breakfast and clearing up the place, it was time to head to the church and set up the reception in the church hall. Kate had to carry everything out there with her, since she would not have time to come back to dress. Dave drove Joe and

Martha out first with the food and wedding cake while Delores worked on Kate's hair. She was done by the time Dave came back. He got dressed in his suit and the rest of us also put on our wedding clothes and piled into the two cars and Dave's truck.

My dress was very nice, light green, with dark green ribbons around the collar and wrists. There was also a band of dark green ribbon at the hem.

We arrived in plenty of time and the hall looked absolutely wonderful! People began arriving, bringing gifts and food. By the time we entered the church, it was jam-packed! I had not expected so many people to come to the wedding ceremony! There were people from Dave's work who showed up with their families. Delores was there with her family, as well as people Mama knew from the store. I realized that anybody who wanted to come, showed up.

I sat between Martha and Joe and the boys sat with Dave's parents. Our group filled the two front rows of the church.

Finally, the service began and I focussed my eyes on Kate as the music started. She looked very beautiful. I also took a good look at Dave, who was very handsome in his new suit. As a matter of fact, I had never even seen him in a suit before. They looked great!

Aunty Martha reached for my hand and held it tight as Dave and my Mama exchanged their vows. John and Maggie stood up there with them and Cindy was the one with the ring on a small pink satin pillow. She looked really cute in her frilly pink dress. It had ribbons and lace around the collar, on the sleeves, and around the hem. Cameras were flashing and going off all through the ceremony. I hoped someone was taking pictures for us to keep. I wanted to remember this day always!

After the wedding ceremony, everyone piled into the church hall and music began to play. People milled about, eating and talking, shaking hands and sharing stories. I had just finished refilling some cups with coffee when I noticed a fur hat between the many heads by the doorway. I loaded up a paper plate full of sandwiches and cake and pushed my way through, and there stood Hitz! I came to a stop in front of him and offered him the plate. He was beaming with joy as he settled down at a table in the corner with a couple of old Native women, who immediately began giggling at his many short comments. I left him to his new company and ran to find Kate to tell her that Hitz had come.

After what seemed like a short time, people began filing out, and soon there was only our group from the cabin. Even Sir James and his sons had disappeared for awhile. Charlie and Milly were still there. I noticed that Milly was talking to Aunty Martha and that Milly was actually laughing. I guessed that Charlie had made things all right. Kate was still rushing about with Gram Marion at her heels. Maggie, as usual, sat quietly sipping her champagne, observing the occupants of the room. When Mary and Martha finally got everything packed away,

Dave had already made several trips back to the cabin.

Joe and Aunt Martha came back with me and the boys to the cabin to get the supper ready while everyone else finished cleaning the church hall. Then Charlie arrived on the truck with Jeff and John and they came in lugging a box. They gestured for us to come closer, and there it was! A television! A wedding gift for Dave and Kate! The boys burst into excited exclamations as Jeff and John got the television unpacked. Charlie and Joe stood there rolling their eyes and Joe said, "Not so fast, boys. You can't just plug it into the wall and turn it on. We're not in the city! There's a lot of work to be done yet!"

They went out and the boys scrambled into their outdoor clothes. They had unloaded some bigger boxes and metal frames from the back of the truck and laid them out on the ground before I realized this was the antenna for the television. I still hadn't got over the shock. A television in our cabin!

I knew immediately what Mama would think. A washing machine would have been better appreciated. We had the wringer washer, but it was still a hands-on, all-day washing affair. Then we went out in the freezing cold to hang up the wet, quickly freezing clothes on the line.

I turned and helped Martha with the loaves of bread she was taking out of the oven. She made wonderful bread.

FINDING GRANDMA

LIFE AT THE CABIN AFTER THE WEDDING WAS VERY strange. Christmas came and went without the usual closeness between me, Mama, Billy, and Cindy. Billy hardly noticed me anymore; he was always with Todd and Henry. Cindy remained pasted to Kate, as I thought of her now. It seemed my own mama was gone; now I looked at Kate, and she was Dave's wife.

Right after the wedding, when the guests had gone home, the new bedroom arrangements brought changes I didn't like. Kate moved into Dave's bedroom and Todd moved into Kate's old bedroom, so that Billy and Henry were now by themselves in the boys' bedroom. Cindy and I remained in our old room. They didn't even talk to me about it.

Why did Todd get to move into Kate's room? It should have been me who got that room! I said nothing and went about my business. And I never sat and watched that silly television that the boys always rushed toward whenever we got home from school. I usually sat in our room and arranged my stuff as if I was going somewhere.

Toward springtime, Dave and Kate announced that they were going to change our names to Dave's last name so that we could all be one family. I noticed that they didn't even look at me when they said that. So I figured I didn't want his name anyway! I wanted to keep my own name, and they were not going to change it. So, while Cindy and the boys whooped with joy, I stood up and faced Dave and Kate. "I have my father's name and no one is going to take it away from me!"

I turned and marched into our bedroom and slammed the door. I sat there waiting for Kate to come in to talk to me and assure me that everything was all right, the way she used to do. She never came. She was not going to be bothered by me. I decided then that I would pack my stuff in boxes and move to Grandma's the first chance I got after school was over.

I made a big show of carrying home from school every day a cardboard box that the janitor saved for me. I told him my mother was packing our old stuff away and needed boxes. I brought the first box home and plunked it on top of the bed and began putting in the clothes that I did not wear every day. Kate walked by the bedroom once, glanced at me, and continued into the kitchen. She said nothing, and neither did I!

After I had gathered about four boxes, I had nothing

else to put away and no one to talk to either. Even Hitz had gone out to his trapline far out in the bush somewhere. I had no idea when he'd be back. Not that Hitz ever said very much, but he was fun to be around.

I began to come home later and later. I took my time getting home from school and hung around at Delores's hairdressing shop more and more often. I helped her sweep the floor and clean up, and once in awhile, she would give my hair a trim or curl the ends of my hair. One day, I was slowly walking home in gathering dusk when I saw Dave's truck go by me and stop. It backed up and I kept walking. Finally, he parked the truck on the side of the road and ran up beside me saying, "Stop! Ray, we have to talk." I did not turn and he grabbed my arm and turned me around.

"Come into the truck and we'll talk. I don't want you going on like this any longer. We've been waiting for you to come around and tell us what is on your mind. Your mother told me to wait, but I'm not used to waiting for someone to decide to talk to me."

He pulled me to the truck and I got in and decided to clamp my mouth shut. He looked at me. "Was it the bedroom?" he asked. I nodded and he sighed. "Henry wets his bed once in awhile, and neither of the boys wanted to sleep with him anymore."

I glanced at him and I saw him smiling at me. I smiled back. "You are kidding."

He shook his head and crossed his heart. I put my

head down. Yeah, that was possible. I did remember my mother grumbling about having to wash the boys' sheets so often. I said nothing as I waited, and finally Dave leaned back on the seat and asked, "What else? The name change?" I nodded.

"Kate said it would be easier to have all the children registered under the same name for the family allowance cheque," he said. "As for me, I'm not ashamed to share my name. I have a very honourable name. One that every child would be glad to own. My name...." I elbowed his side. I knew he was going into one of his made-up plays. All right, I guessed that made sense.

"I don't want my name changed, though," I said.

Dave sighed, "I know. You said so, and we did not change it. You have a right to keep your name. Now, what else is the problem?"

I shrugged and leaned back into the seat. "I don't belong here. I'm too old and I'm a girl."

He thought for a moment. "If we moved into town and we had a bigger house so that you could have your own room, would you be happy then?" he asked.

I hadn't thought of that. To have my own room? But I would still feel like an outsider when I saw Dave and Kate together, including in the kitchen where I used to be...that was it!

I turned and looked at Dave and, after taking a deep breath, I spoke softly, "I think I don't like you beside Mama all the time where...I used to be. I think that's all.

And...I don't know if I will feel different later...will I?"

Dave sat there looking down at his hands in the dark interior of the truck. "You're very smart to understand that, you know that? Not very much escapes you, does it? No, maybe not soon. You still feel like I took your mama away from you. You don't even call her Mama anymore, do you? When did you start calling her Kate? About the time we got married, wasn't it?" I nodded.

"What would you like to do about it?" he asked. "What is it that would make you happy?"

I did not hesitate. "I want to go and stay with Grandma. I want to live there with her and help her. She needs me. Kate doesn't need me anymore. I feel like I'm just in the way, like someone that just lives there."

Dave sat still for a few minutes longer before he said, "Can you wait until school is over? Stay until school is out, and then you can go to your grandma's place again for the summer. In the meantime, we'll figure out how we can arrange it so that you can go to school there. Remember also, that your grandma is an old lady. What will you do if she gets sick?"

"If she gets sick, it will be better that someone is there with her than for her to be all alone as she is now." I replied.

He turned and looked at me. He was smiling. "Your mama is going to kick me, I think. She doesn't want you anywhere out of her sight, you know. She always looks down the road and starts pacing the floor until she sees you coming down the road. I have found her many times, sitting on your bed looking so sad because she cannot understand why you are not happy...but enough of this. Let's go home. You okay now?"

I nodded. I hadn't realized I was worrying Kate. I just thought she didn't care when she didn't try talking to me. I had to remember that Mama loved me and always would.

Springtime came with sheets of rain and thunder! The snow disappeared almost over one weekend, and by Monday morning, we trudged off to school, feet splashing in streams of mud running down the middle of the road. Cars and trucks drove by amid sounds of screeching girls as they dodged the muddy sheets of spray.

School continued to be not a bad place to spend the days. I learned a lot and enjoyed listening to my school-mates in the cafeteria at lunchtime. The girls loved to gossip about people in the town. This provided some sort of entertainment, but I always remembered not to repeat what I heard. It was something that Grandma had told me I must never do.

I tried my very best to remember all the things I had learned when I was with Grandma. I wished I could see her now. Hitz had come home before the ice disappeared. He was the brownest Whiteman I had ever seen! He looked like a potato with white gouged-out eyes, and ears that poked out of long strands of grey hair that stuck out beneath his big beaver-skin hat. Oh, he was a sight for sore eyes! I had missed him very much.

FINALLY, THE GRASS, LEAVES, AND FLOWERS came into bloom. I listened to the sounds of noisy frogs coming through the open window and then the noise from the nesting birds. I knew it wouldn't be long before I saw Grandma again. Hitz and I went bike riding several times, but now, most of the time, I had no idea where the bike was. The boys had gradually taken it over.

I counted the days to the end of June, and finally school was out! It was almost lunchtime, and I ran home and packed the last of my things into my suitcase and waited for Dave to come home. I was getting very nervous. Dave was late, very late. If he didn't come home soon, I was going to miss the train! I said nothing as I glanced at the clock on the wall for the hundredth time.

Finally, I heard the truck pull in. When he came through the door, he glanced at me, then stood still for a moment before he walked by without a word. He should have called Grandma to tell her I was coming. What was the problem? I said nothing and sat at the kitchen table, still patiently waiting for him to come back into the kitchen. Kate was by the stove packing their lunch. They were planning on driving out to the lake and having lunch there while the boys went swimming. I had no intention of going, since I was getting on the train this afternoon.

When Dave came back into the kitchen from the back porch where he had gone to wash up, he sat down across from me. "I called and your grandma is not there. The storekeeper I talked to said something about Grandma being with your Aunt Vera."

Before he could say anything more, I rushed into my bedroom and closed the door. I was totally devastated! I was all packed to leave right now! I had even changed my clothes! I was ready to burst into tears when I became very quiet. I could still go. Grandma would return from wherever she was. She would come home and I would be there waiting for her. But I knew there was no way Kate would let me get on the train when Grandma would not be there to meet me. I shoved the suitcase under the bed and lay down, wishing they would all leave soon so that I'd have time to run down to the train station to buy a ticket on time. I had enough money saved from my winter's work.

Soon Kate came in with Dave behind her. "We're going now. Are you coming? We'll keep calling Grandma every day until we know she's there – then you can go, all right?"

I lay there looking at them. No, there was no way I was staying here waiting for Grandma to come home. "That's okay. I don't want to go to the lake today. I'll just lie here a bit and maybe go see Delores later," I said.

Kate nodded and they turned and went out. I could hear Dave calling the boys and then the truck door slammed and the engine started. By then, I was at the window watching the truck pulling away and then they were gone, down the gravel road.

I ran into my bedroom, grabbed my suitcase, and stopped to scribble a note to leave on the kitchen table. It read, "Gone to Grandma's. I will wait for her there. Don't worry. Love, Ray." I went down the road opposite to the way Kate and Dave had gone and ran as fast as I could. I hoped no one would notice me.

I slowed down at the corner where there were more and more houses. Finally, I came around the corner to the train station. I ran the rest of the way and entered the station, heading straight to the ticket counter. The man didn't even glance at me as he handed me the change and the ticket. It was no more than ten minutes before the train came around the corner. Wow, that had been close! If they hadn't left when they did, I would not have caught the train on time. I got on the train without looking back and settled down on the side I would be getting off on.

It seemed like an awfully long time before the train gradually slowed down nearing Grandma's place. Then we came around the corner and there was the lake, the cabins, the store, and the station. I grabbed my suitcase and stepped off the train. There weren't many people around, just an old couple and several kids, because it was just pouring rain!

After the train had gone, I hurried down the railroad tracks and found Grandma's path turnoff. I slid on the gravel slope off the railroad tracks and managed to get my balance as my foot landed on grass at the bottom. I ran down the path with huge dripping leaves hitting and swiping me right across my face and body. I was totally drenched by the time I broke through the bush and saw the back of the cabin.

I slowed down as I approached Grandma's cabin, and I saw immediately that there was no smoke coming out of the stovepipe. Slowly I came down the path, so disappointed and now afraid, because I had never considered what I would do if she had gone to live at Aunty Vera's place for the summer! To my further dismay, I saw a padlock hanging on the wooden door as I came around the corner of the cabin.

Where had she gone? I put my suitcase down and considered what I should do. It was around the middle of the afternoon, nearing supper, because I was suddenly aware that I was very hungry! If I did not figure out how to get into the cabin, I could end up sleeping outside, maybe over there by the stack of firewood. I shoved my suitcase under the square washtub overturned against the side of the cabin and sat down to figure out what to do.

The rain had stopped and the sun came out. After about ten minutes, I thought I would wander down the path and ask if anyone knew where Grandma had gone. The canoe! If her canoe was not there, then I'd know she had to be around the lake somewhere! I took off at a run down the path to the landing, but the canoe was gone. Now I knew she was still around, but where? I ran to her next-door neighbour, Sarah. But Sarah was not home when I got there.

I next ran to the store and found that it was open and people were still there, milling around. I asked a woman if she knew where my grandma had gone. She glanced at me and then turned to take a good look at...my eyes. She looked at a man in the corner of the room and I recognized him as Sarah's husband. I approached him quietly and asked, "Do you know where my grandma has gone? My name is Ray."

He turned and looked at me, while appearing as if he was sorting out some humongous mountain of information in his brain for about two whole minutes, before he said, "Yes, I remember you, Green Eyes. You are soaking wet."

When I didn't respond, he continued. "I think one of her daughters arrived...oh, one or two days before...they went camping somewhere...I think one of the Section men said he saw them at Mile Three portage."

I nodded and ran out. I turned to go back to the cabin, but then stopped. What for? I didn't have anything in the suitcase that I would need right now. I just had a couple of shirts and pants in there and all kinds of other stuff like driftwood, rocks, and braided grass. No, I would be wasting time.

So I took off along the railroad tracks heading east, setting up a steady jog until I got beyond the curve, out of sight of the community. Suddenly, quietness descended on me. I heard my breathing and my pounding feet on the railroad ties. Ravens squawking to my right, then the constant hum of flies on the flowers and plants along the railroad tracks.

Soon I came to the Mile Two portage. I was pretty proud of myself for being able to run non-stop for so long. I seemed to have got my wind, but if I had to change my pace or footing, I found I would have to start all over again until my breathing became normal as I found my running speed.

I was getting into a kind of a rhythm again when I heard a train coming. Oh, shucks! I slowed down. I had to get off the railroad tracks to wait for the train to go by, but suddenly, my heart skipped a beat! Oh, no! There ahead of me on the left-hand side of the sloping rocks leading to the tracks, was a large mother black bear with two little cubs trailing behind! They were no more than half a city block ahead of me! What was I going to do?

I stopped frozen still, then ducked behind a bush beside the tracks, my mind scrambling as to what to do! The train was coming from the west, I was going east, the bears were heading east. I could not turn back! I saw the train's headlight come around the corner and heard a loud blast of the whistle. I made my decision then.

I had enough of a shoulder to run on for quite a distance on the right-hand side of the tracks. The bears were on the left-hand side. I stood aside to wait for the train engine to go by and then I ran as fast as I could, with the train whipping by me at full speed, banging and crashing, in smashing gusts of wind soaked in smoke and wheel grease. I thanked my lucky stars that this train seemed to go on forever. By the time it had gone by, I glanced back. I had got quite a ways ahead of the bears, but I could still see them, milling around the same spot where I'd seen them. They must have stopped to munch on some berries or something.

It seemed as if I had been running non-stop for a very long time when I got a whiff of campfire smoke. I slowed down and realized I had reached the portage at Mile Three. I couldn't decide if the smoke came from the left or right side of the tracks until I actually saw the canvas tent top on the right-hand side. I walked slowly forward. I did not want to seem to arrive in a panic. I nonchalantly wandered into the campsite, just as Grandma was coming out of the tent with a pot full of blueberries.

"Naens! What are you doing here? Did you come in today?"

I smiled and nodded. "Yes, Grandma, I got off the afternoon train and Sarah's old man said you would be here." She was now all over me, giving me a kiss on the forehead and hugging me.

I sagged against her, and suddenly a feeling of relief swept over me. I nearly burst into tears, until I saw my aunt Vera coming up the path with a string load of fish. I realized that they were alone. Aunt Vera had left her brood behind. She had four little noisy, boisterous, mischievous children. Two little girls and two little boys. I smiled. I pitied their father, who must be looking after them now. Vera was nice. I loved my aunty Vera. Her face, too, broke into a smile when she saw me.

"Ray! You got here by yourself?"

I nodded. I was very proud of myself and tried to appear as brave as I could. I went to help Vera with the fish, holding them while she snatched some pine branches from the pile by the fire. I set the fish down on the branches while I answered their questions as fast as I could. After we had cleaned the fish, Grandma handed me a cup of tea with a chunk of bannock and a bowl of blueberry jam.

Then she sat beside me. "Did your mama call first before you got on the train?" she asked.

My chewing stopped and I slowly swallowed before I nodded. "Dave called. They knew you weren't home." I took a sip of tea.

"You got on the train by yourself without them knowing." It was a statement. I nodded. She took a deep breath and said, "You thought...what?"

I looked at her and said, "I left a note for Mama and...I thought I would just live in your cabin until you came home. How was I supposed to know you had a big new padlock on your door now?" She smiled and shrugged, but said nothing more.

Just then, I noticed Vera gathering the fishy branches and fish guts. "I passed a huge mother bear with two cubs coming this way. They might be here before dark," I said.

She stopped and looked at me. "You walked by a mother bear with babies?"

Grandma also stopped and looked at me, shaking her head. "If you say you weren't scared, I will definitely know there is something very wrong with you."

Vera asked, "How did you manage to get by them?"

I finished chewing my last bite of bannock and jam. "Remember the train that went by? I stopped and waited until the train engine went by before I ran like the dickens and got way, way past the bears before the caboose passed me. Was I scared? Yeah, I nearly peed my pants when I first saw them, because I didn't know what to do, besides staying out of sight, until I saw the train coming."

Vera started giggling, shaking her head. Grandma said, "Better put those branches and fish guts as far as you can on the other side of the tracks. They may just decide to go right past our campsite. Unless one of those little cubs gets curious. Just like little kids, those things. They're the ones that get you in trouble, most times."

I had just thought of something. "Grandma? Why didn't we come here last summer?"

Grandma looked at me. "Because while we were camped by the shore across the lake, there was a full-grown wounded bear wandering around here – got hit by a train."

"Did they ever find it?"

Grandma reached for a stick to poke the fire with and replied, "Oh, it arrived at the community in the fall –

right after you left, as a matter of fact." Boy, she was really making me dig the information out of her!

"Did they kill it?"

"Oh, yes. The dogs chased it to the open field in front of the store and the men shot it."

I couldn't help feeling sorry for the bear. It wasn't his fault that the train came by when he was crossing the tracks, was it? I wondered if he was related to the mother and cubs back there. Why didn't Grandma tell me about it last summer? I decided not to ask any more questions. Grandma didn't like being asked about things she didn't volunteer to tell you in the first place.

We had just finished a supper of fried fish and managed to get everything put away before another rainstorm hit. Grandma kept the candle lit for a long time, while the thunder and lightning crashed over us, and then it began to get farther and farther away. I awoke to the sound of Vera breaking branches and I looked right at Grandma's closed eyes when I opened mine. I was all snugly warm inside Grandma's blankets. I smiled and slowly traced my finger over her forehead to the tip of her nose. She didn't move, but her eyes were slightly open. Then she made a face and stuck her tongue out at me.

THE BEAR

SUMMER 1981

WHEN VERA AND I WERE ALONE FOR A FEW MINUTES the next day, I told her I was sorry I had interrupted her stay with Grandma. Vera laughed.

"I'm very glad you came, Ray. Kate and Mother always got along very well. Martha and Mother...well, Martha being a bit bossy always irritated Mother, because she couldn't order her around as she could with me and Kate. Now, Mother and I...well, we kind of bore each other, I think, after more than two days anyway."

I shook my head. I could not imagine Grandma being bored with anyone. "Why would you think that?"

Vera just shrugged. "I just can't seem to think of anything to say to her and she, being as she is, I mean, she never says much anyway. You know, you're just like our Kate. Maybe that's why Mother likes you so much. You take the time to think about what she has to say. With me, 'poof!' It's gone out of my head the minute she's finished talking. Now, tell me more about Dave." I sighed. That was all she wanted to talk about. She had not met him yet either.

I realized I wasn't much shorter than Vera, so I got to wear one of her skirts while I washed my shirt and skirt and hung them over some branches to dry. I still wore my one-piece slip, which I would then wash with my panties once my shirt and skirt were dry.

The sun was very hot that day and into the next. Grasshoppers buzzed endlessly in the shimmering heat beyond the rails. We wasted away the afternoons, floating in the canoe beneath the quiet shade of the rock cliff. Grandma trailed a fishing line attached to an inch-long hook with a chunk of bait stuck to it. She managed to catch at least one fish every day.

We had a couple of flat cardboard boxes of blueberries already. By Monday, we would have to get them to the store to sell and then Vera would also have to get back to her children. After that, I had the whole summer with Grandma!

Monday came and we were already at the store. The storekeeper poured the boxes of berries into baskets and paid Grandma for them. Vera went home with a couple of jars of blueberry jam and four little canoes I had carved for her kids. When the train was gone, Grandma and I walked down the railroad tracks, hand in hand, in complete silence.

As we came around the corner of the cabin, I looked

at Vera's jeans hanging on the line. She had washed them and left them for me. I didn't wear jeans very often, in fact I could not remember when I'd worn jeans. I usually wore the stretchy pants with elastic around the heels if I wore pants at all. I preferred my skirts in the summer — they were much more comfortable and I didn't have to wear socks if I didn't want to. Grandma saw me looking at the jeans and she said, "They will be better to wear for walking through the bush."

I glanced at her as she pushed the door open. "Why would I want to go walking through the bush, Grandma?" She smiled at me and did not reply, like it was her own little secret. All right, I could be patient. I said nothing as I watched her pull her clothes box from under the bed. I also pulled out my suitcase and my box of camping clothes I had stored under the little bunk bed where I slept.

Still she said nothing as she began repacking the box and left a pile of clothes on the bed. I knew now that she was ready for a long trip. I piled my camping clothes to the side too, then threw the rest that I had outgrown into the suitcase and shoved it under the bed. Next, she pulled out the packsacks, into which we stuffed our clothes.

We already had the bedding and tent packed, so Grandma started packing several more pots. I began lugging all the packed things outside, because it seemed like we would be leaving immediately. I stood in the doorway as I watched her pull her kerchief over her head and tie the ends into a knot under her chin. I said, "I know, we're going to cut wood for the stove. That's it, isn't it?"

She turned to me as she shoved the jar of mosquito repellent into her pocket and grinned. "No. We are not going out to cut wood."

I tried again. "Are we going far away up north to fish and pick berries?"

She shook her head, no, as she pulled the door behind her and snapped the padlock on. I took my packsack, grabbed whatever I could carry in my hands, and trotted off to the canoe in front of her, while I debated where we could be heading. I met her on my way back to get another load and said, "We're on our way to deliver babies for some people who are camping along a lake someplace."

She flicked me on the arm with her bag as she passed me. "No. Don't forget the jeans. They're still hanging on the line."

I ran up the path, giggling. After swinging the last packsack on my back, I took the pants off the line and stood back, looking around for something we might have forgotten. The axe! Ha, she would be glad to see that. I picked up the axe and headed back to the canoe.

As I neared the landing, she had already finished loading up the canoe. She saw the axe and smiled at me. "You will never, ever, guess where we are going. Now, answer this question and explain why. Do you want me to tell you where we are going, or would you like to find out when we get there?"

I loaded the last packsack into the canoe and got in while she held it steady. I stuck my paddle to the bottom of the water while she got in behind me. Then we floated free. We paddled through the creek and out to the open lake. I paddled steady and deep as I thought about the question. After about half an hour, I spoke.

"If I don't know where we're going, I won't know how hard or fast to paddle; I won't know if I should pee before we get into the canoe; I won't know if I should drink lots of water; I won't know if I should eat a big meal before we go; I won't know how to prepare for the trip...."

There was no response at all behind me. So I continued.

"Shall I paddle to save my energy and make sure I don't build up blisters on my hands? Or, if it's a short trip, I could paddle in spurts and fool around, then paddle hard for awhile before I drift off watching the seagulls again. And if I don't know where we're going, I won't know what to anticipate. Are we going to see someone? If we're going to see a whole bunch of people, then I don't want to be wearing those baggy jeans!"

I paused and waited. Still there was no response from her.

"If I don't know when we're going to reach where we're going, then I might just be wearing my slip when we come around a point right into a camp full of people. If I don't know we're going to a camp full of people, then I might not eat so much when I could have eaten all my food, knowing that they would feed us when we got there...."

Finally, Grandma said, "All right, enough already!"

But I continued, "If I don't know...."

Suddenly, a huge sheet of water landed squarely on my back and splashed up to the back of my head! Still holding my big gasp of breath, I felt the canoe shaking as Grandma sat back there, giggling. Lifting my paddle, I plunged it into the water sharp and hard and was rewarded with the sound of a sheet of water hitting an object behind me. I heard Grandma sputtering and I giggled as I continued to paddle.

After awhile, Grandma said, "Remember the portage I pointed out to you last summer, off to the right, and just at the tip of that bay that runs around the point there?" I nodded. "That's where we're going to portage over to another lake. It's a small lake, so it will feel like only fifteen minutes or so before we have to get out and portage again. The lake on the other side is longer and it will be night by the time we get there. We will sleep there overnight. Maybe even stay there a day or two. It is close to the big rock cliff by the railroad tracks from there, and I hear there are huge clumps of blueberries there."

I glanced back when she stopped talking. She was lifting her paddle, allowing the water to run down the length of the paddle and into her mouth. I smiled. So, we were going blueberry picking along the railroad tracks to the west of the community. But why all the supplies?

She cleared her throat and continued. "After that, when we have filled the case of jars I brought with blueberry jam, we will continue our journey. There is another portage we go through and then we will follow a swampy river right out into a larger lake. At the other end of that lake stands a cabin on the right-hand side. We will probably reach it in late evening. I would not want to camp anywhere before that. It is rather swampy and muddy and will be full of mosquitoes."

She paused again as I waited to hear whose cabin it was or who lived there. After she had another slurp of water, she said, "Joshua will be expecting us. That is where his trapline is."

So we were going out to visit Joshua! I turned to look at her and said in as close an imitation as I could of Joshua's voice, "Agnes, Old Woman, it is times like this that...." She rocked the canoe so suddenly, I nearly lost my balance! I grabbed the sides so fast I nearly dropped my paddle! I could hear her softly laughing behind me and I decided to start paddling again, now that I had a purpose and a destination.

We took our time going through the portage. I made two more trips after we carried the canoe over. I had a bit of a problem, though, when we went to put the canoe down at the other end. It was very muddy and my running shoe sunk into the mud. When I went to step back, my shoe came off, and there I stood on one foot with just my sock on the other foot. Grandma laughed and said I looked like a muddy one-legged crane. Somewhere in the mud was my shoe! She peeled off a big chunk of bark from a downed pine tree and threw it at my feet, and that was what I stepped on as she threw a branch to me.

I dug around in the mud until I was able to reach the tip of my shoe and pulled it out. Strangely, the inside had no mud. Whatever fell in, I was able to dump out. So it was all right and I put it back on. When we pushed the canoe into the water again on the other side, sure enough, the wet sweaty hair on my forehead had only cooled off before the canoe slowed down at another clearing in front of us. This too had a muddy landing.

I jumped out and pulled the canoe up as far as I could before Grandma stood up. She was right, the flies found us almost instantly. Blackflies swarmed around our heads, so thick I felt them crawling around my ears and eyes. Grandma dug into her pocket, pulling out the mosquito repellent and wiped a big dollop of it in my hand. I rubbed both hands together and shut my eyes tight as I rubbed the repellent down my face, throat, ears, and neck. I wiped the rest on my hands and up my arms as high as I could reach.

It was incredible – we were almost choking on the blackflies, they were so thick! I ran back and forth to the other end of the portage with the packsacks before we picked up the canoe. It was hard carrying the canoe, because there was nothing you could do if you got a bite. You couldn't let the canoe go to swipe the flies away.

Well, getting sweating hot and putting on mosquito repellent did not go together. The stuff ran into my eyes with the sweat and, next thing I knew, I was wiping my eyes with my shirt or anything I could get my hands on.

"Blow into the spot of the shirt in your hands before you wipe your eyes with it," Grandma said.

It worked and, almost instantly, the stinging was gone. Finally, the canoe was in the water and loaded and we paddled away from the flies.

The lake was large, dotted with many small islands and bush-topped clumps of rocks. As we came around the first island, I noticed a huge black cloud coming up over the horizon. Grandma dipped her paddle deeper at the same time as my paddle dug into the water a little quicker. We would have to hurry and find a place to camp. Around another point, there was a perfect campsite, and Grandma steered the canoe into the small sandy bay amongst a thick stand of short cedar.

We had just set up the tent when the rumble of thunder echoed over the hill. I ran and chopped pine branches for our bedding as quickly as I could, while Grandma set up a makeshift table she had found by a pile of blackened campfire rocks. It looked like the campsite was used quite regularly, perhaps by duck hunters in the spring. We rushed to get our things inside the tent.

After I had finished depositing a thick layer of pine branches inside the tent, I noticed that Grandma had stretched a plastic tarp over her makeshift kitchen. On the table sat our teapot and our other little cook pots, including a small pot full of blueberries we had picked at the first portage. I had just managed to throw the wash basin over the blueberry pot before the first downpour. We laughed as we huddled just inside the tent flaps. We had managed to turn the canoe over and get the food box into the tent in the nick of time.

The rain came down in sheets as darkness descended. We dug into our food box and found half of a pan-sized bannock along with a jar of blueberry jam. There was some moose jerky and a pouch of pemmican. We opted for a bowl of pemmican each with some lard I melted in the little pot over a candle Grandma had lit. The candle now sat on top of the wooden food box as we ate. Every once in awhile, a loud clap of thunder would make us jump, and once I bit my tongue when lightning struck rather too close for comfort!

We dipped our bannock in the blueberry jam and laughed at each other's stained bluish-black teeth and mouths. Still the rain came down and soon I needed to go outside to go to the "bathroom." But there was no let-up. Finally, with much laughter and teasing, Grandma pulled out a green garbage bag she had stashed underneath her fishnet and this she cut open and draped over me. I ran out and did my business under that plastic bag, then returned to tease her as she tried to cover her larger form underneath it.

I watched her hurry out, and we kept up a bantering

conversation in between the horrendously loud claps of thunder and near-bright-daylight lightning that lit up the night sky. When we had managed to get our bedding in order, Grandma lit another candle to alert the thunderbirds of our location, so that they didn't strike us by accident. We settled down in our bedding and she started telling a story about lightning and thunder and what had happened to some people during a storm like this.

She had no sooner started the story when, in between the claps of thunder, we heard our pots banging and clanging outside. Grandma grabbed her flashlight and both of our heads popped out of the corner of the canvas tent door. As another flash of lightning lit the ground, we saw a huge black bear, up on his paws on top of our table!

"Hey, go away! Get off of there!" Grandma yelled.

This was a stone-deaf bear, it seemed, because it didn't pay any attention to us. I joined in with Grandma's yells, in English – in case he didn't understand Ojibwa.

"Yeo! Bear! Beat it! Get lost! Buzz off! Vamoose! Shoo!!!"

Suddenly, we saw the huge beast take his two big paws off the table in another sheet of lightning. The light shone on the whole area around our campsite. The bear turned and looked right straight at us and started to swing his head left and right. Grandma drew a tight, quick breath and clamped the tent flaps down quickly.

In a flash, she had whipped the shotgun out of its case, which she had leaning against the back tent wall.

She always carted that gun around with us whenever we went camping. I had got so used to it, that it was just something else we had to cart around. Then she was rummaging around her bags almost frantically, before I realized she was looking for the shells!

We had never taken the gun out of its case, let alone used it, and I just then remembered that I had thrown the leather shell bag into the...fish tub. Only because I didn't want it to get wet! She had told me once that we had to keep the shells in a dry place at all times and since it was going to be raining and...anyway, the shells were outside, safe and dry in the fish tub under the overturned canoe down by the shore.

Grandma had just dived to a packsack at the back of the tent before I reached her. I put a hand on her arm and yelled over another clap of roaring thunder. "I threw the shell bag in with the fishnet inside the tub and it's under the canoe! I didn't want the shells to get wet!"

She stopped suddenly as we waited for the next flash of lightning. It came with such a sizzling closeness that we could actually smell the sulfur. Then we crept to the front of the tent again, slowly lifted the flap, and waited for the next flash of lightning. It came, but it showed no bear in sight.

Grandma blew one candle out. Since we might have to keep a light on all night, we didn't want them burning out too soon. Another hour seemed to creep by with no let-up of the storm. Just when we thought the storm had gone by and our candle was now only a little stub on the baking powder can lid, we were about to relax and go to sleep when a mighty swipe sent all our pots and pans banging and clanging to the ground!

We jumped up and Grandma turned her flashlight on and I, for some reason, dove for the light and covered it with the blanket, hissing, "Shut it off! Shut if off! It will see us!"

She hissed back at me. "He knows we're here! He already saw us and he can certainly smell us! He can also smell the bacon and eggs, meat, and fish we have in the food box in back of the tent! Well, I am not about to give him any of my food! He can just dang well go find his own!"

Just then, there was another huge crash outside! We peeked out just as a flash of lightning shone over the whole campsite, and we saw that he had decided to swipe the frying pans off the tree where we had them hanging! I noticed that the pot of blueberries under the washbasin was still sitting on top of the table undisturbed. The bear was nowhere around.

Grandma decided she was going to have to go outside, walk down the path to the lake, and fetch the shells from the fishnet tub under the canoe. Oh, I did not think that was a good idea! I finally persuaded her to wait until the thunder and lightning had passed and then we would both go down. But no sooner had we agreed than we realized that the storm was not over yet.

Another thundercloud was right above our heads.

This time, it was much worse than the first one. We could hardly talk in the ensuing cracking of lighting and earth-vibrating thunder! Suddenly, the whole side of the tent shook and four claw marks ripped the left section of the tent! Rain immediately poured in as it flowed over the middle tent pole. This time, shock and fear washed over me and I started to tremble.

I had not realized how tense I was, knowing that the bear was outside. I grabbed Grandma's sleeve and yelled over the noise of another clap of thunder, "Is he going to eat us?"

She turned to look at me and smiled. "Naens, that bear would puke up its guts if he ever got a taste of you!" I could feel my eyebrows lifting up as she continued.

"He's not interested in us, it's our food he wants." Oh.

Grandma jumped up and grabbed the flashlight. She set the food box right in the middle of the tent and lit all of our last four candles in a row on top of the food box. Then she took the gun, clamped a hand on me, and yelled over the noise.

"We will walk to the canoe together, load up the gun, and come back up, and if the bear is anywhere in sight, I will blast it to pieces!"

I was shaking, scared so badly I could hardly walk. Another clap of thunder made my heart skip a beat as we stepped out of the tent. Sheets of lightning lit our way down to the water. Grandma yanked the canoe up and I reached under and pulled the shell bag out of the fishnet tub.

Another shattering streak of lightning shook the ground beneath us and sheets of rain poured down. Grandma shoved the shell bag somewhere under her shirt and we hurried back up the path with her arm linked in mine and the flashlight bobbing between us.

When we got back to the campsite, there was no bear around as another thunderbolt shook the ground, followed very closely by another sheet of lightning. We hurried into the tent and actually giggled from the release of tension as we once more slapped the tent flap down and wedged it with a rock inside.

Grandma loaded the gun and laid the other shells in line, in case she needed them. Feeling a bit more secure, we smiled at each other. There was nothing we could do about the long rips in the tent where water was now pouring in. We were just beginning to relax again, as the thunder and lightning seemed to be receding in an easterly direction.

We figured it must have been about four in the morning when our makeshift table sticks actually bounced off the tent wall! The bear had sent the whole thing flying toward us! Grandma lifted the tent flap and I was right behind her, with our candles almost burned to the quick behind us.

The round glow of my flashlight settled right on the huge bear who had just lifted his head from the spilled pot of blueberries on the ground. His front paws lifted off the ground and he took a short hop toward us with a loud grunting noise. Suddenly, Grandma's shotgun went off! Right beside my ear!! I shut my eyes tight and fell back against the inside tent flap. I felt my body shake as another clap of thunder shook the ground. A glance showed me that the bear had fallen no more than a metre in front of the tent.

Grandma immediately pulled the tent flap down and wedged it shut with a rock. There was absolute silence outside after that. Yet I was keenly aware that we were also held prisoner by that thing lying dead outside our door. I crept close to Grandma as she lay down on her bedding, and she held me in her arms as we listened to the storm rage, rumble, and crack until early morning.

When I awoke, Grandma was not there beside me. I sat up quickly, then heard her outside humming at the same time that the green branch smoke came to me. I took my time pulling my shoes on and straightening up the bedding. When I stepped out, the bear was gone from the front of the tent. I saw the plastic tarp she used to wrap the fishnet now lying over the dead bear. She had covered it. I did not wish to see it.

Grandma had already packed our breakfast and lunch into a cardboard box, and it appeared she was only waiting for me to get out of bed. After I had gone to the "bathroom," she was already by the lake waiting for me. I hurried down and got into the canoe.

We paddled around a small point where, right above the bay, lay the railroad tracks, already shimmering in the morning heat. We left the canoe below the railroad tracks and sat down to rest under some shady bushes. We didn't wait long before the Section men came by on their way out to check the west track.

I watched the little yellow putt-putt car come around the bend. They slowed down and Grandma was there talking to them. After that, we set about picking blueberries. Just before lunch, the little putt-putt car came back again and Grandma said they would tell the one family back at the community who ate bear to get it off our campsite before we came back that evening.

After the men had gone, we headed farther west toward the huge rock cliff that Grandma had heard was loaded with blueberries. Sure enough, we found lots, loaded thick and big. It was getting on late afternoon when we headed back to the canoe. I noticed immediately that it had been moved.

Grandma said nothing as we loaded the blueberries. We pushed the canoe out and Grandma even got a couple of fish by trolling back and forth across the mouth of the bay before we headed back to our campsite. We had wandered several miles down the railroad tracks this afternoon, so we would not have heard the people if they had come and picked up the bear. So the first thing I did when we came to the shore by our campsite was to run up, and sure enough, the bear was gone. Even Grandma's tarp was gone. She did not like that too much. But I didn't care. The bear was gone!

JOSHUA

T HAT EVENING, AFTER A MEAL OF FRIED FISH, WE MADE blueberry jam from the berries we had picked and poured the jam into the hot jars and sealed them. I had just come up with a pot of water from the lake when I saw Grandma melting a wad of wax in a little dipper.

"What are you doing?" I asked.

She glanced at me. "Well, I certainly had not planned on burning all my candles at once as I did last night, so now we don't have any more. So I decided to melt all these little candle stubs and stick a string from my bag in the middle of the wax and make a new candle."

I sat down to watch. When she had melted the wax enough to mould without it being liquid, she flattened the wax in between her hands and shoved the string in the middle, folded the sides, and rolled it. It looked like a thick white cigar with a string sticking out. When it had hardened enough, she set it down to flatten the bottom.

There it sat, wobbly, finger-dented...and crooked. I sputtered in laughter and decided to get away from there before she did something to me.

When she was done, she came and sat down beside me on a sloping rock by the water and we watched the sunset. It was so calm and peaceful. The air was fresh and the birds sang...and then a train went rumbling by. It sounded very close in the evening stillness. That kind of killed the moment. We looked at each other and decided to get to bed, for the mosquitoes had suddenly descended on us for their evening meal. We were very tired from having stayed up most of the night before; we didn't even bother lighting up Grandma's crooked candle.

The next morning, we packed up and loaded our things into the canoe. We left the case of blueberry jam in the sealed jars, nestled under the shade of some bushes. We paddled very slowly and softly, as the world around us was still very quiet. There was not a breath of wind and the lake lay shiny as a mirror. We talked barely above a whisper as we rounded another point of land.

There in front of us, a large moose emerged. It stopped by the shore and looked directly at us. Right behind it came another smaller one. It was a baby! It too saw us and we must have been so interesting to the baby moose that its long legs didn't have time to slow down before it crashed into its mommy's behind. Its head jerked to the side and the mama moose turned her head to look at it, as if she was saying, "What's the matter with you, watch where you're going!" I turned and smiled back at Grandma. We drifted right by them, and later I turned to see that they were in the water now, having a drink and cooling off in the morning sun.

By noon, we came upon the portage. We took our time getting the canoe and all our things across to the other side. When we had finished loading the canoe again, we stopped and munched on the morning's left-over fish and bannock. It was very hot and I didn't feel like doing much of anything else. I just wanted to get back out on the lake where it was cooler. But in front of us was a swampy, windy river.

The river was flanked by scraggly tamarack trees and there were many, many white water lilies surrounded by lily pads bobbing on top of the waves we made. It looked like a field of white flowers on lawns of green. We turned left and then right down the winding river for what seemed like miles.

Finally, after watching a few more blackbirds with the orange-striped wings and turtles sitting like little flat stones on top of floating logs, we came out into an open lake. Since you couldn't drink swampy river water, I was very thirsty by then. When we finally saw the opening, we paddled out quick, like we were just released from a sling-shot. Just then, a bit of wind came up and, oh, I threw my head back and let the wind cool off my sweating head.

Now we paddled strong and steady across the lake.

When I thought it would be near suppertime, we came around an island and there was the end of the lake. The bay was rimmed with a narrow strip of sand beach and there, to the right, was a log cabin.

As we paddled nearer, we saw that there was no smoke coming out of the stovepipe. Seeing that it was such a hot day, we wouldn't expect it to be smoking anyway. At this time of day, though, someone should be cooking supper by now, but there was no one in sight. I turned to Grandma. "Does he know we're coming?" She smiled.

"Sure he knows. I said we'd be here around the second week of the month. Why? Do you think I should have telephoned him first?"

I made a face at her. "No, he'd probably have just jumped on the train anyway." I looked around the unspoiled, undisturbed wilderness and hoped that nothing from the outside would ever make its way out here. This place was at least two days travel to the nearest telephone or railroad.

The canoe gently nudged the sandy shoreline and that was when I noticed Joshua's canoe turned over beside a low shrub cedar bush. We got out and lugged our things to the cabin. It was unlocked, so Grandma pushed the door open and we brought our things inside. It seemed very dark in there, coming in from the bright sunlight. The room smelled of woodsmoke and cedar. I noticed a small clump of cedar branches on the table. He must use them as a hot pad for his pot, I thought.

Grandma went back out while I waited for my eyes to adjust. I saw a double bed in one corner beside a window, covered by a very brightly coloured checkered quilt. Shirts and coats hung from nails on the log walls above the bed. That must be where Joshua slept. Another double bed on the opposite corner beside another window had only a bare mattress. I put our bedding and clothes on top of that.

There was a teapot on the stove by the door and, putting my hand on it as I went by, I found it was still warm. There was a smaller window above the table beside the door. The place was very neat and tidy.

Grandma had just turned around from the campfire when I came out. "The ashes are hot. He must have gone somewhere near."

We had just turned the canoe over and picked up the rest of our things when Joshua came around the corner of the cabin with two partridges dangling in his hand. I noticed that he carried no weapon. No gun, no sling-shot, nothing. He said, "I thought I heard voices. So, here you are." Joshua was talking to Grandma as he came toward us, but something caught my attention behind him.

There it was! I saw a small black thing come around the corner of the cabin, but it ducked back again. A puppy? Did Joshua have a puppy? Why was the puppy so shy? I thought a puppy would have come running, bouncing and barking for attention. I waited, and sure enough, it stuck its head out from around the corner of the cabin and slowly it lay down on the ground and rested its head on its front paws. I smiled and asked Joshua, who was now kneeling by the campfire, "Who's your little friend?"

Grandma had been rummaging around in our food box, and now she turned and stopped still, looking at the little puppy. Joshua looked up at me. "Little friend?" He turned and he too stopped still. My glance caught Grandma's tension as her eyes swept the area beyond the cabin and she, in a soft voice, said, "Go into the cabin and stay there, now!" Joshua had also stood up and gradually moved to the left away from the cabin and I still didn't get it!

What was going on? I walked to the cabin door and toward the little puppy, but it stood up and shied away, disappearing around the corner. That was when the realization hit me with a shock. That was not a puppy. It was a baby bear! I went in and closed the door. What if the mama bear was behind the cabin where we couldn't see her?

I stood around inside the dark cabin. There were ceiling beams above, moss-chinked walls, and the odds and ends of clothes hanging on nails on the horizontal wall logs. Joshua, I noticed, had no pelt stretch-boards or fur stretchers hanging inside the cabin. They must all be hung up outside somewhere, I thought.

Grandma came in, lugging the food box. I moved to

the side window and saw Joshua slowly walking along the edge of the clearing. He moved out of range behind the cabin.

"He didn't even know he was being followed, silly old man." There was laughter in her voice, and I turned to see her looking out the other window. I could see her shoulders shaking as she softly giggled. I failed to see what was so funny.

"What if the mother bear is out there looking for her baby?" I asked.

Grandma turned around. "The question is why that little cub followed him in the first place. If the mother was out there, she would have called already, and the cub does not appear to be calling for its mother either."

By now, I could see Joshua walking along on the other side of the clearing, still searching the ground. Just then, at the front window, the little cub came into view by the campfire. It stood waiting for the approaching Joshua. The cub sat down by the campfire and proceeded to slowly scratch its belly, lifting its snout to sniff the air.

Grandma came to stand beside me and we watched Joshua approach the little cub, saying something. Then he knelt down in front of the cub as he continually glanced around the area.

The cub rolled to its side and lay in the soft grassy ground.

"Do you think he's sick?" I asked.

Grandma said, "He is very small and skinny, and

looks very weak. He certainly hasn't been eating enough food. He should be bigger by now."

Joshua pushed the door open and wedged it wide with a piece of wood.

"I have no idea where he joined me on the trail. I have never seen bear tracks in the area. There are no...." His voice trailed off as he pulled out a can of condensed milk from the cupboard. "There is the tourist camp by the railroad tracks. But that's about two days travel from here. The tourist spring bear hunt may have killed his mother, but how could he have survived so long on his own? He looks pretty bad."

Grandma pulled a bowl from the cupboard, while Joshua punctured the can and poured the milk into the bowl. I stood by the window, watching them. They seemed to have totally forgotten about me.

She said, "He wasn't very far behind you. He either walked or ran to keep up with you, in which case you should have heard him, or you walked by where he lay sleeping."

Joshua moved the can back and locked his eyes on hers, and I saw his eyebrows rise nearly to his white hairline. "Are you implying, Old Woman, that I am getting deaf and blind in my old age?"

Grandma pursed her lips and I could tell by her dancing eyes that she was ready to go into another giggling fit, but she kept her face straight as she moved her face to within several inches of his. "I am just saying, that you didn't hear it, you didn't see it, but there is now a baby bear out there waiting for you to take care of it."

Joshua leaned back from her, took the bowl of milk, and went out. We stood by the door and watched him kneel beside the cub, talking to it and dripping milk from his finger to its mouth. Suddenly, the cub sat up and we heard it slurping as it lapped up the milk. I decided to go fetch some tall grass and pine branches for its bed.

By the time Grandma finished making our supper inside the cabin, I had a neat, round, thick, soft bed ready for the cub outside the cabin, between the corner and the door. How to get the cub there was another question. Joshua still had not made any attempt to touch the cub. It now lay in the shade of the bush beside the campfire.

The sun was now behind the treetops. Joshua's cabin faced the rising sun out on the open lake, but he would never see the setting sun because of the hill and the trees behind the cabin. The cub did not pay any attention to our coming and going as we got ready for bed, and we made sure we did not disturb him where he lay beside the campfire.

The next morning, Joshua was just coming in when I woke up. He got a fire going in the stove and I could hear the soft drizzle of rain on the roof. I did not want rain, not today. I wanted to examine the cub.... I propped up on my elbow. "Is the baby bear still there?"

Joshua smiled and nodded at me, and he gestured for me to come have a look. I slept by the wall, so I scam-

pered to the foot of the bed, for Grandma was still asleep, or had been asleep – she was now up on one elbow watching us. I went to the door and poked my head out. There, on the soft bed I had made for him, lay the bear cub, all curled up snug and warm with its nose tucked somewhere in its paws.

His bed was sheltered by the overhanging roof at the front of the cabin. I smiled at Joshua. He indicated the bowl on the table, and I poured the rest of the canned milk into it. When I peeked around the door, the cub was sitting up on its bed looking at me. Slowly, I put the bowl down on the ground beside the door and stepped back inside. Soon, there came a slurping noise as he licked up all of the milk.

Grandma got up, and while I fixed the bed, she went outside. I saw her walk by the window on her way to the outhouse. I looked around the door and saw that the cub had gone back to bed and the bowl was licked clean.

I picked up the bowl and the baby bear didn't even lift his head. When Grandma came in, she said, "Hmm! He may as well be a little black fur ball for all the interest he has in us." We had partridges and dumplings for breakfast and Fur Ball's bowl was also filled. It sat, cooling off, while we ate our breakfast.

The rain came down steadily all day and the wind picked up. I decided to do a bit of carving at the table while Grandma swept out the place. I had slept like a log all night and did not hear the mouse party that had apparently gone on all night which Grandma was complaining about. Joshua had gone to check the fishnet out on the lake. I sat at the table facing the window, which gave me the full view of the lake.

Joshua was in relative shelter from the wind, since it was coming from the south. I watched his canoe, hugging the southern shore of the lake. From there, he moved along the shelter of an island and disappeared to the other side. Fur Ball still lay curled in his bed after he had gobbled up his breakfast.

My carving slowly took shape in my hands as the pile of wood chippings grew on top of the table. I didn't realize what I was carving until I looked at the round shape of wood in my hand – Fur Ball.

Grandma was quiet now, but I could smell the mosquito coil she had set to burn on top of the window shelf. The door was still wide open and it brought the mosquitoes in. It was too dark in here with the door closed, and besides, it was very muggy-warm.

I turned to look behind me and saw Grandma sitting on the bed looking at the backs of her hands, then slowly turning them over. After awhile I said softly, "You knew it was going to happen one of these days, didn't you? You knew that one day you would wake up to find that someone had switched hands with you during the night!" Gee, I didn't even get a chance to move before her bag landed on the back of my head. That was when Fur Ball appeared at the open door.

Grandma moved fast and was at the door before he could move. "Not so quick," she said. "No way, you are not coming inside! Go on now, stay outside. Out you go!" The cub shied away from her waving hands and disappeared around the corner. I went to the side window and watched the small form slowly walking on the path toward the trees with its head down in the pouring rain.

"You chased him away, Grandma. He's probably crying now. See how he's walking, rejected, like nobody wants him. Poor Fur Ball."

Grandma laughed from the doorway. "Oh, that's right. Feel sorry for him. What you have to remember, Naens, is that Fur Ball is a wild bear. If he keeps eating like he's doing right now, by next week he'll be the size of a dog, and by next month he could carry our canoe for us over the portage, if he had a mind to."

I giggled. "Oh, Grandma!" She jerked her head to the window and my eyes followed hers, and there was Fur Ball doing his business...by the outhouse.

We laughed as we saw him turn around and come back to the cabin with a purpose to his steps. I threw a piece of bannock on his bed, and when I stuck my head out the door later on, he was on his back with his paws crossed at his chest. He had white hair on his belly. I hadn't known bears had any white hair on them at all. Just then, I spotted Joshua coming along the shoreline.

After Grandma cleaned the fish Joshua brought back, we had fried fish for supper and Fur Ball had a bigger meal in his bowl – the same size as the piece of fish I had! Joshua was gradually increasing the food he was giving him. Again, Fur Ball tried to come in, but Grandma was not having any discussions about that.

She was the first to touch him, as she literally turned his whole body around and pushed his butt out the door. There was no let-up of the rain and I listened to it steadily dripping off the corner of the cabin outside. There had been nothing much to do, so we had gone to bed early. I couldn't sleep though.

I turned around, facing Grandma. I thought of Fur Ball. What was he going to do when he got well and strong enough? Would he stick around or go back to wherever he had come from? What if he didn't ever leave? He'd grow to be a big bear. I flipped around and faced the wall. Joshua would be here, living with a big bear. What would Fur Ball do if people arrived to visit Joshua? Would he attack them? Would he get mad at Joshua if the old man didn't have food to feed him? Would Fur Ball kill Joshua and eat him?

No, Grandma said, black bears were not interested in eating people. I turned around again. Maybe Fur Ball would bring Joshua some food if the old man had nothing to eat. But what was Fur Ball going to do when Joshua went to the community to get supplies? He couldn't follow him back. The dogs would go crazy and the people would probably shoot him. The thought immediately brought back the image of the marauding bear Grandma had had to kill. I turned around again.

I wondered what was going to happen. When winter came, he'd have to go sleep in a cave somewhere, wouldn't he? Where was he supposed to find a cave? Would Joshua have to go out and find him one? Joshua stayed in this cabin in the winter to trap, so Fur Ball couldn't sleep in here. What if Joshua built him his own little cabin? Maybe it wouldn't be warm enough though. Maybe Joshua would have to dig a hole against the hill over there.

I turned around again. Suddenly, Grandma nudged me with her elbow, whispering, "Go to sleep, you! If it's not the mice, it's you turning around with your sharp elbows and knees...."

Then Joshua was up on his elbow, whispering, "What's the matter? You hear something?"

Grandma muttered, "No, it's this girl thrashing around like she's got ants running around inside her pants!"

I curled up against the wall and giggled into my blanket. I willed my muscles not to move and tried to blank out my mind. The more I tried, the more words came out in my brain: talking, talking about not talking, and then talking about the talking.... Hey, the rain had stopped. I listened to the stillness, Grandma's gentle breathing, and Joshua's exhaling breath that had a short sharp whistle attached to it at the end...and then came the soft scratching at the door.

It sounded like Fur Ball was rubbing himself against

the door. Poor thing. Slowly, I got up on my elbow. Grandma's breathing did not change. I carried the folded blanket I used for a pillow as I edged my way to the foot of the bed. Quietly, I moved across the floor and nudged Joshua's coat aside from the door. Slowly, I pushed the latch up and opened the door a crack. I knelt down and instantly touched a wet nose.

I opened the door a bit more and then Fur Ball was right against my chest. I shut the door softly and curled up on the floor beside the door, pulling the blanket around me. Fur Ball did not hesitate as he nestled himself against my chest and belly. His back was to me and his damp fur wafted up my nose. He stank! He smelled like wet chicken. If he was going to be so close to me, he was in for a good scrubbing tomorrow!

DECISIONS

I SOON DISCOVERED MY MISTAKE WITH FUR BALL. I HAD allowed him to nestle against my chest that first time, and now that was where he flung himself every time I got near him at that level. That first morning, when we were rather unceremoniously ejected from the cabin, he was always at my heels. I needn't have worried about Joshua and the bear, it appeared that the problem was now mine. What was I going to do with him?

Grandma and I had decided to take the canoe and go blueberry picking one morning. My thoughts went back to the bear cub. I put my paddle across my lap and looked back. Fur Ball sat by the shore where the canoe had been, patiently waiting for us to return.

We had been here for two weeks already, and he never let me out of his sight. He followed me everywhere I went, and he stayed by the shore every time we went somewhere in the canoe. What was he going to do when

Grandma and I went back to the community? I would have to go home soon too. No, he would have to bond with Joshua. That meant that I had to stop playing with him and running around with him. He was just like a little puppy.

Grandma suddenly stopped paddling. I had no idea how long I had been sitting in the canoe with my paddle across my lap, thinking. I glanced back. "I have to stop playing with Fur Ball. If he's going to stay around Joshua's cabin, he has to think Joshua is his mama. Otherwise, he may try to follow us and...we don't want him where we're going."

There was no response for a long while and I waited. Finally, she said with a sigh, "A pair of moccasins. I was just wondering where I was going to get the leather to make a pair of moccasins. I used up my last piece this spring. I do have a sheet of moosehide that's dried raw, but I would need help with it...."

I sat rolling the paddle back and forth on my lap before I asked, "How did we get from Fur Ball to a pair of moccasins?"

I heard her laugh behind me and she said, "I made a bet with Joshua that you would come to this realization last week. As you see, I lost. So now I have to make him a pair of moccasins."

I glanced back, smiling. "Serves you right. What was he going to do for you if you won?"

She replied, "He was going to make me a new pair of snowshoes."

I asked, "What's wrong with the ones hanging against your cabin wall?"

She answered, "Actually, I couldn't think of anything else he could make for me."

My thoughts went back to Fur Ball. "How am I going to get Fur Ball away from me if we're around him all the time...?" I had not finished speaking before I knew the answer. We would have to leave. Her next words were:

"We'll leave tomorrow. The food we brought will last Joshua to the end of the month, providing Fur Ball doesn't eat him out of house and home. After that, well, Joshua will have to figure out how to get to the community and back without that bear. Since Mother Nature will knock Fur Ball out for the winter, Joshua can go about with his trapping this winter. Springtime, now that will be interesting."

We paddled to the island where we had found a lot of blueberries several days ago. We had filled all the jars, so we were now picking to eat and to fill up Fur Ball's never-ending appetite.

On our way back, we paddled slowly, enjoying the scenery. I didn't know if I would ever see this place again. I tried not to think about having to go back home. I knew one thing – I would much rather stay with Grandma. But I said nothing about it. She knew how I felt and whining was not an option – definitely something one should never do.

As Joshua's place got closer, sure enough, there was

Fur Ball, curled up at the canoe landing, waiting. He was pacing back and forth long before we were even close enough for him to hear us. Joshua had arrived from his wanderings in the bush. He pulled the canoe up and laughed as Fur Ball jumped into my lap after he knocked me down.

The next morning, we said our goodbyes silently with not even a wave. Joshua was sitting on the bank at the edge of the sand beach, holding Fur Ball in his lap. They were still there when I looked back one last time before we went around the point. From there, we paddled quietly but with a purpose – to get to our destination before nightfall. Back to the campsite where Grandma had killed the bear.

We arrived, and everything was exactly as we had left it. The wooden table was still wedged tightly between the trees and our tent poles were there waiting for us. I brought the case of blueberry jam and deposited it under the wooden table. We didn't speak as we went about setting up the tent for the night. After a meal of leftover fish and bannock, Grandma decided that we should set the fishnet for the night.

We paddled out to the channel and set our fishnet, arriving back at the tent just as it was getting dark. We were quite tired when we finally curled up in our blankets.

The next morning, there was not a cloud in the sky. We hurried before the land got too hot. Grandma went and got the fishnet while I packed up the tent and camp stuff. She came back with six fish that we cleaned before we loaded up the canoe. I hated the thought of the muddy, mosquito-infested portages ahead of us.

Throughout the whole day, we rarely spoke as we hurried through the portages and paddled across the lakes until, finally, we emerged at Grandma's lake. We were home. We could even hear the dogs barking from the community in the late afternoon stillness. Grandma smiled at me as we finished loading the canoe.

"You know? There is no reason why we should hurry back to the cabin. Why don't we camp over there at that island? We'll check out that blueberry patch by the railroad tracks tomorrow, eh?"

I grinned back. That was a very good idea. We paddled slowly to the island and took our time setting up the tent. After pulling up the canoe, we lugged the food box into the tent and set up our bedding. It was so wonderful on the island – no mosquitoes! I was sitting on a boulder facing the setting sun when I noticed an unusually loud splashing behind me. I got up and looked over the outcrop of rocks, and there was Grandma, floating around in the water by the sloping rock.

That was a good idea! I didn't even hesitate as I pulled my one-piece dress over my head. I kicked my shoes off and pulled off my socks and I was in the water with Grandma. I hadn't quite got the hang of swimming, since I was never anywhere near a lake in my younger days, but the last couple of summers had given me the opportunity to float around. Grandma usually just had her bath by the shore without actually going into the water. She didn't know how to swim either.

Now I pushed myself off into the deep, and after some initial splashing and mouthfuls of water, I was swimming! Grandma laughed and squealed as I swam around her and splashed her each time I came near.

That was the beginning of my swimming experience. I soon learned to dive. I would stand at the high rock cliff and dive into the cool water. When we went along the railroad tracks to pick more blueberries, I couldn't wait to go swimming on the other side of the tracks. This side of the portage was in a swampy, muddy bay. It was good only for muskrats, moose, and bloodsuckers.

After another week of camping, Grandma looked at me one evening and said, "Do you know what day it is today?" I shook my head and I felt my heart sink. It was time to go.

The next morning, we made our way back to the community. I paddled very slowly and took a long time memorizing the shoreline. Grandma managed to hook a large trout on our way back. That was a lot of excitement! We looked forward to having trout for supper!

When we got to her boat landing, we unloaded the canoe and carried our stuff up to the cabin. Nothing was disturbed. We opened the cabin door and it smelled very stale inside. I wedged the door open as I ran back for another load.

Grandma was at the campfire getting the fire going when I got back. I had no sooner got our stuff unpacked and was ready to fill up the teapot, when I heard someone talking outside. I looked out the window and saw our neighbour walking away with the big trout swinging from his hand. I hurried outside.

"Your mother apparently called early this week," she said. "She wants me to call to let her know when you are coming home."

I said nothing about that, but I sat down beside Grandma and smiled at her. "Okay, now, Agnes, Old Woman, what are we going to have for supper?"

She smiled. "Well, let's get cleaned up. Wash your hair and change your clothes. Then we will go to the store, call your mother, and buy some pork chops for supper, eh?"

After some bannock and tea, we headed to the store. When we got there, I walked in behind Grandma and closed the door behind me. There were seven people in the store and I noticed that they all looked at me a little longer than necessary, but I felt the twitch of a polite smile on my lips as I met each one's stare. I had gone a long period of time without being stared at, and I was just now reminded of my weird looking eyes, and very loudly in the silence!

I examined the cans lined up on the shelves as I waited for Grandma. The storekeeper rang the number for her at the telephone, and soon I heard Grandma talking and then she was beside me. She got pork chops, bananas, and some canned fruit. We headed back out and had gone quite a ways along the railroad tracks before she spoke.

"I told Kate we would be arriving on the train tomorrow." I glanced at her and smiled. So she was coming with me! Tomorrow morning. We still had tonight.

The next morning, we got up rather late and took our time having breakfast and getting our things together. She stood by the bed looking at me as I packed my clothes and the things I had brought with me.

"Leave those," she said. "Take your suitcase back home empty. Take only the things you need."

I glanced at her. Did she think my clothes were too small for me now? Or was she going to make sure I got new clothes when I got back home? One thing I had already packed inside the cardboard box that I shoved under the bed was Aunt Vera's jeans.

All too soon, we were walking along the railroad tracks, making our way to the train station. We hadn't been standing around too long when we heard the low rumble of the approaching train. Soon the headlight came around the corner and I became aware of my heart beating against my rib cage. I did not want to go back!

I stood still, not saying a word as I waited to follow Grandma up the steps and into the coach. We took our seats and I gave Grandma the money I had brought with me. She took it with a twinkle in her eye. What was she up to? I just knew she was up to something! But I was afraid to ask. We sat beside each other, not saying much as we waited for the train to stop at our destination.

I must have dozed off, because Grandma was shaking me. "Come on, get your things together. We're here." Already? I rubbed my eyes and got up behind Grandma as the train lurched to a stop. We got down and Dave was there to help Grandma to the ground.

Kate came rushing forward, grabbing me in a big hug before I could put my suitcase down. What was the excitement? She had never done that before. Now Dave was in front of me with his hands on my shoulders.

"Wow! Look how dark you are," he said. "And tall! She must have grown half a foot taller, wouldn't you say?" He glanced back at Kate. Then the boys and Cindy were all over us.

The train pulled away as Dave got all the bags and kids into the back of the truck. I had just turned to head for the truck when Grandma took my elbow.

"Look by the corner of the station," she whispered. "There's an old man there that looks like someone is flagging his body out of the corner of the building once in awhile."

We waited, and sure enough, the man's body stood out then swung back behind the building again. "Flagging him out," she said. Well, he did look like someone was using his body to fling out like a rag. I giggled and walked to the corner.

There was no way in the world I would miss that

beaver hat! I stopped at the corner and waited, and suddenly, there he was in front of me. I threw my arms around Hitz and his arms closed around me. It was a full minute before I felt his body stiffen, and I knew Grandma was standing behind me. He stepped back and I could see that he was exactly as he had been the last time I'd seen him.

He looked me up and down before he said, "You grown up." I pulled Grandma over and introduced her to Hitz.

Grandma's eyes filled with laughter before she nodded and said, "So, you are the famous Hitz. She speaks about you often."

Hitz cracked his toothless smile and looked almost embarrassed as he brought up his shoulders, which touched the tips of his hair jutting out from under the beaver hat. He shoved his hands into his pants pockets and stood there rocking back and forth. Yes, he looked quite pleased.

Dave called from the truck, "Ready to go!" We waved to Hitz as we hurried to the truck. Grandma climbed into the front with Dave and Kate, as the boys pulled me up with them at the back of the truck.

I noticed the flower garden along the walkway as we pulled up to the house. We had never had a flower garden before. It was nice! We spent a nice afternoon visiting and sharing stories. We told about the bear in the thunderstorm and about Fur Ball and Joshua. Grandma told the stories so wonderfully, I laughed as if I hadn't been there and was hearing them for the first time. That evening, they decided I was to sleep with Cindy on my bed and Grandma would sleep on Cindy's. When Cindy went off to bed, there was a lull in the conversation, so I decided to go to bed too. I hadn't realized I'd missed her so much. Cindy seemed very shy with me this evening. When I had settled down beside her, I told her about the baby bear and how he felt in my arms. With amazement in her voice, she asked what his eyes looked like and how big his teeth were. We giggled, whispered, and talked for a very long time. When Cindy drifted off to sleep, I realized that there must be a serious conversation going on in the kitchen. Their voices droned on and on, with periodic lapses of silence.

It was late when I awoke to Grandma banging into the corner of the bed and heard her gasp. I lifted my head. "You okay, Grandma?"

She whispered back, "Go to sleep. We'll have a very long day tomorrow." I lay back down, but it was a very long time before I went to sleep.

The morning started with a noisy ruckus in the boys' bedroom. Someone was bouncing a ball against the wall. Boys! Boys! I swung my feet down to discover that Grandma was already gone.

I got dressed and entered the kitchen. They were all sitting there looking at me. Grandma, Kate, and Dave. Grandma looked like she had won something in a raffle draw. Dave had a pleased grin on his face. Kate looked like she had lost something. I stood there a moment before I said, "Okay. Let me think...Grandma caught a rabbit, Dave cleaned it very nicely, and Kate...burnt it in the oven."

Dave glanced at the others before he burst out laughing. Grandma put her head down and Kate looked at Dave, but she did not smile. This was serious. I took a cup from the cupboard and the coffee pot from the stove. No one said anything as I filled up their cups and poured coffee into my own cup before I returned the pot to the stove.

I could feel their eyes follow my every move. I sat down at the table between Grandma and Kate and facing Dave. I put some sugar and milk into my cup and slowly stirred it as I waited for someone to tell me what this was about.

Finally, Kate took a big breath and said, barely above a whisper, "I have told my mother that you may go and stay with her this winter."

Shock went clear through me! I realized I had locked my eyes on Dave and he was slowly nodding his head at me. I turned to my mother and said, "Thank you, Mama." I glanced at Grandma and I could feel my heart pounding against my chest. To calm myself, I continued.

"I promise I will look after your mother to the best of my ability and should she ever.... Ouch!" Grandma had kicked me on the shin! They all started laughing.

I looked at Mama and understood how much I loved her. I turned to Grandma, thinking how can two people – a mother and a daughter – be so very different? Kate was always so serious. She was always thinking. Always in the silence of her own thoughts...like me, perhaps?

I smiled. I was happy, happy! I was going away for the winter! I was going to live with Grandma! Wait till I told Hitz! Poor Hitz. He wasn't going to like this. He was going to be very lonely. Who was going to talk to him and go bike riding with him? Maybe he would be at his trapline most of the time anyway. Come to think of it, he'd never used to be around much until I started spending time with him.

Grandma and I spent the whole day going to second-hand shops and the church rummage sale, picking out clothes made of strong material that could be made into pants, blouses, and dresses for me. We even found a winter coat that fit me just right! I had also discovered that I could no longer fit into the clothes I had packed away in the cardboard boxes. How had Grandma known I'd have this problem?

When we were at a second-hand shop, I was aghast when she shoved five of those slingshot things at me. Bras I mean. I hadn't thought about things like that. I did realize, of course, that my shirts were getting tight. What a nuisance, just the same!

Then Grandma marched to the laundromat with jingling coins in her pockets. We shoved the stuff into a large washing machine and she made me sit still the whole time while they finished washing. Then I read the instructions for a huge dryer into which we shoved the whole wad of wet stuff. We turned it on and sat down to wait, facing each other across a small table.

I found myself looking at her expressionless face. I was determined that I was not going to make any facial movement either as I stared back into her eyes. She didn't move her face, but sat perfectly still. After a long while, I was sure half an hour had already gone by, but still we did not move. I would not be the first!

There were just the two of us in the whole place, and when it appeared that there was not going to be a winner, Grandma suddenly hitched herself to the side and let out an explosive blast of gas! Her eyes were still fixed on me as I doubled over in helpless laughter. "Cheat!" I gasped. "That was cheating!" Then the dryer buzzed. I got up and called the taxi as Grandma bundled the wash.

When we got home, the sewing machine was pulled out to the living room, and Grandma and Mama set to work, with a lot of snipping and buttons flying. I left the room and went outside to bring more wood in. I looked around the clearing. The boys had trampled all the grass with their boots under the tree where the swing was gently going back and forth in the breeze.

They had gone off with their slingshots somewhere and Dave had taken Cindy out to get some treats for after supper. I was not going to miss this place though.

Somehow, I had never felt like I belonged here. I was sad about Billy. He paid no more attention to me than Todd and Henry did. He was my brother. He would always be.

I went back inside and began to pack the few things I could still fit into. My baggy sweater now fit just right and my long pleated skirt with the elastic waist also fit perfectly now. I had bought something for Grandma when she wasn't looking at the rummage sale. I paid twenty cents for them. I was going to save them for Christmas. I pulled them out now and laid them flat on the bed. Two tams. One red and one blue. And they had the little spike thing on the top too! She just had the black one that she always put on when she was going somewhere. It lay on top of Cindy's bed where she had set it down when we returned. Now, she would have three. I folded my sweater over the two new ones and packed them in my suitcase.

After supper, Grandma and Mama came into the bedroom with an armful of things for me to try on. I had three blouses that fit just right. Three skirts that were a bit too long, but they looked nice. One full-length dress. I hadn't seen that one before. Mama said she had bought it for me when the new things arrived at the rummage sale. And there were two pairs of pants that had been cut down from the waist to the ankles.

All in all, they were very nice. I would have new clothes to wear for school this winter. Grandma left the room and Mama was still kneeling on the floor folding up the hem of my pants, telling me that I would grow into them shortly. I reached down and touched her shoulder.

"Thanks, Mama. You sew really nice."

She looked up at me with tears brimming in her eyes and put her arms around me. Her head came up against my chest and I stood still, stroking her head as she held me tightly. Her hair was very soft and I trailed my fingers down it.

"I love you, Mama. Are you sure you're going to be okay?"

She sat back, wiping her eyes. "Yes, Ray. I will be okay, baby. I've packed a stack of stamped envelopes in your suitcase. Write to me often. Never forget also that you are your father's daughter and that I love you very much." I realized just then, that every time she looked at me, she would remember my father. She had told me often enough that I had his eyes.

I flopped down in front of her and we sat eye to eye and I told her the whole scene about the staring match with Grandma at the laundromat. I was right in the middle of imitating Grandma's gas explosion when Grandma appeared at the door. Mama and I hugged each other as we rocked in laughter. All too soon, it was time to go to bed, and again I had trouble getting to sleep. I was too excited!

After another hectic morning, we made it to the train station right after lunch, and there was Hitz again. This time, Grandma didn't follow me when I joined him, way at the end of the ramp by the tool shed. I asked how he knew when we were leaving and all he said was, "Charlie." He hugged me, kissed my forehead, then looked down at the ground and turned to walk away.

I didn't know what to say. Suddenly, he reminded me of Fur Ball, the way he had walked away, totally dejected and forlorn in the pouring rain.

"Wait! Hitz!" I called. "I made something for you." I ran up to him and reached into the pocket where I had shoved my carving of Fur Ball. I pulled it out and put it into the palm of his hand.

"It's a bear cub who came to live with us in the bush. His name is Fur Ball. He was all by himself...."

Hitz stood looking down at the carved wooden bear, curled in the palm of his hand, before he lifted his head and looked at me. "You did this, Ray? You made this?"

I nodded my head, beaming. "Yes, Hitz. I love to carve."

He looked back down, saying, "It is beautiful, Ray. And you made it for me?"

I'd had no idea who I was carving it for at the time I made it, but here it had been, still in my pocket, and now there it was, cradled in the middle of his hand, right where it belonged. So, yes, I guess there was only one person I made it for. I smiled at him. "Yes, Hitz. It's for you."

I heard Mama calling for me from the station. "Wait, Hitz. What is your mailbox number?"

He lifted his head and smiled. "Oh. Well, that is not important, you know...."

I knew he was about to go into one of his rambling talks that could go on forever, so I asked again, "What is your mailbox number? You see, I would like to write to you sometime. Would you like that? I know you can read."

His face lit up and he gave a mirthful, toothless grin. "Yes, yes! You write me letter. H'it's hun'red sixty, six, at the post office. Good!" I stood there wondering if he'd said it correctly. He sounded like he was stuttering, but then there was no way I could stop the giggle that accompanied my words as I gave him a quick hug.

"Okay, one, six, six. I'll write you a letter. Take care!" I turned and ran toward the train station as the engine came rumbling by me.

The train ride seemed to take forever, and when the train finally stopped at Grandma's place, there was our neighbour waiting to help us with the two extra cardboard boxes that held my clothes and things. For his trouble, Grandma gave him two jars of blueberry jam when we reached the cabin.

I felt like I was coming home for the first time in many, many years. We unpacked and cleaned up the cabin a bit before we stopped by the stove. We had just realized we had nothing to cook for supper. I didn't feel like going back to the store and it was too late to go set the net for tomorrow. The pemmican! Grandma smiled as I grabbed the pail and headed for the lake.

When I came back up with the pail of water, she was by the campfire with a sizzling pan of bannock, a bowl of pemmican at the side, and a pot of blueberry jam heating by the fire. We weren't going anywhere, so we were going to stuff ourselves with blueberry jam and laugh at each other's blue teeth!

We settled by the fire after our supper. We grinned with our blue teeth at each other once in awhile. Suddenly, a figure materialized past the trees on the path, coming toward our cabin. We sat waiting, unmoving, trying to figure out who it was. He was dressed in black. He wore a long, flowing coat of some kind.

Grandma drew a quick breath and she whispered, "Gracious ghosts, that's a priest!"

A what? I sat up. I didn't think I had ever spoken to a real live priest in all my life! I whispered, "What's he doing here? I didn't know you had a priest here."

Grandma glanced at me. "There is a Catholic church there by the lake, but he hardly ever comes here. Let alone, to my cabin!"

I took a deep breath and lay back on my backrest against the woodpile, and just above a whisper, I said in my best Joshua imitation ever, "Oh, Agnes, Old Woman, you done something real bad, now the good priest has come to chase the devil out of you and...." Suddenly, she flicked her fire poking stick and sent a live ash flying right on top of my shoe! I scrambled to get it off just as the priest stopped in front of us and knelt by the fire.

He smiled. He looked about the same age as Dave. He had a kind face. What you could see of it, anyway, for he had a mustache and a beard. He introduced himself, and Grandma nodded and smiled her blue teeth, but she didn't say anything. The priest hesitated and then asked if we had seen Joshua. He had been led to believe that Joshua was Catholic and would be pleased to meet with him.

Grandma smiled and nodded again. That was when it dawned on me. She was pretending not to understand English! I was mighty tempted to say something about Grandma's...condition, but decided that would not be the best thing to do. So I offered the information.

"Joshua isn't here right now and he may not be back until late in the fall, and then probably for only a short time before he has to go back to his trapline."

The priest looked at me for the first time and his eyes settled on mine. Yes, I could see what he was thinking. He'd know that I was a "half-breed" because of my green eyes. I excused myself and got up, heading to the cabin.

At the door, I turned and asked, "Would you like a cup of tea?" I could see Grandma's shoulders sag in relief. Had her going, didn't I? I smiled as I took a cup down and went back to the fire.

The priest sat with us for a long time, until it began to get dark. He was new to this area and he spoke of all the villages and towns that he had travelled to and some of the accommodation problems he had encountered. I laughed at some of his stories. He left with a promise to return for a visit the next time he was in the community. Grandma seemed irritated, because she had missed out on the conversation, pretending she couldn't speak English!

I had found her crooked candle and I lit it while she was gone to the outhouse, and left it sitting in the middle of the table for her to see when she got back. I left the cabin to douse the fire with the last of the water. Grandma always had fresh water in the morning.

I heard her enter the cabin and I went to the outhouse. The flies were now gone. Several dogs were barking way out at the point somewhere. The air smelled very nice and clean. The leaves had already turned yellow and orange.

The next morning, we got the cabin rearranged and did some more cleaning. Then we turned to the work outside the cabin. We stacked up the firewood and banked up the sand all around against the first two foundation logs. Then I fixed the step by hammering on another piece of board to support one that had rotted off.

When we had finished building a shelter for the woodpiles, we decided to go get more wood. It was the dry wood we would need to stockpile. The green wood we could cut from the hillside and pull home on the toboggan in the winter. So off we went. We camped at our favourite camping spot on the island, and we cut and sawed the logs to size, so we could stack them inside the canoe.

After three days out there, we had stockpiled enough wood to last us all winter, so Grandma said. It took us four trips to bring it all back. From the landing area, it took me several days to get the wood up to the side of the cabin, where we piled up the logs. The dry wood was not heavy. I had no trouble carrying the logs one by one.

About a week later, we got a message to call Mama at a new number that was left with the storekeeper. I talked to Mama myself and she had great news. They had moved to a house in town. The rent was not bad and she was now working at Delores's hair shop. Cleaning up and such while Delores was teaching her. She also told me that there were forms she had to sign so I could go to school in the community. I hadn't thought of that. I was to talk to the teacher and go to school here.

Grandma took the phone next and I could tell Mama was repeating the conversation again, with the additional piece of information that the family allowance for me would be sent to Grandma for my keep. We walked home in silence. I was scared. I was afraid of what it would be like, going to school here. I hadn't met any of the kids yet, although I did see some of them at the store. No one had made any effort to come and talk to me.

I said nothing to Grandma. I hoped things would untangle and work themselves out all by themselves. I didn't want to think about it. I was going to make popcorn tonight. I clutched the bag of popcorn I had bought at the store.

When we got home, we sawed more of the wood and stacked it. At suppertime, we took a break and ate by the campfire. It was getting chilly in the evenings now. Soon we would have to eat inside. Finally, when we were ready to settle down for the night, I made a big show of getting the stove going hot and took the pot down and put some lard in it. I put the pot on the hot stove and waited for the lard to heat.

Grandma sat patiently waiting on her bed. I had promised her a new treat sensation. When the oil was sizzling, I poured about half of the bag of popcorn into the pot and dropped the lid on top. Soon the popcorn also began to sizzle and crackle inside and suddenly there began an explosion inside the pot.

I was just putting the popcorn package away in the cupboard when I saw Grandma out of the corner of my eye, reaching for the lid. I said, "No, Grandma, don't!"

Too late. Missiles of popcorn shot out in all directions and one smacked Grandma right in the middle of her forehead before she ran to the bed, yelling, "Take it off! Take it off the stove before it catches on fire!"

I grabbed the lid and threw it back on the pot and the popcorn kernels began crashing themselves against the lid in greater fury. At one point, it looked like they were all ganging up on the lid, trying to lift it up when I pushed it back down. Suddenly, they were all quiet in there.

I took the pot off the stove and set it on the wooden block on the table. I sighed a mighty big sigh and pulled off the lid. A waft of the most delicious smell you ever smelled in your entire life filled the room! Grandma came, crunching on the popcorn on the floor with her feet. She looked at the popcorn and reached for one. She popped it in her mouth and chewed.

I dumped the popcorn into a bowl, melted a bit of butter in the still hot pot, and poured it over the popcorn. I sprinkled salt on it, then I took the bowl to the middle of Grandma's bed and sat waiting for her. She came over with a smirk on her face and sat down beside me. Slowly we munched on the popcorn until we got thirsty. After that, she began a story that went on well into the night.

It was a cold, damp morning and the air was filled with browning vegetation when I got a whiff of smoke from the west. I went down the path to where I could see Joshua's cabin, and sure enough, I saw a spiral of smoke coming out of his stovepipe. I ran up the path and entered the cabin. "Grandma, he's back! Joshua's home!"

She was sitting at the table, cutting slices off a slab of bacon. I could tell what she was thinking when she continued to slice off more than we normally ate. I pulled a jar of blueberry jam out of the box and dumped its contents into a pot on top of the stove. By then, Grandma was rolling bannock in a bowl. We were having company for breakfast! I wondered if that included Fur Ball. I hoped not. The dogs would be at his neck ready to tear at him if he ever showed up in the community.

Sure enough, the bannock had just left the pan and the bacon just finished sizzling when the door opened. Joshua came in and settled himself at the table. As we ate, he told us stories about Fur Ball that got us all laughing so hard. He had reinforced the training that Fur Ball was to wait by the cabin whenever Joshua left in the canoe. Joshua said that the last time he looked back, Fur Ball was still sitting in the same spot by the campfire pit. He was sure he would stay there until Joshua got back.

As to the question of where Fur Ball was going to hibernate for the winter, Joshua had taken Fur Ball on walks, hoping the bear would remember where his den was, but Fur Ball wasn't interested in looking for anything at the moment. He was just tagging along for the walk. One thing Joshua discovered, though; Fur Ball was absolutely not the animal to have with you when you went hunting for moose. It seems there was no way he could get close enough to a moose for a good shot. The moose would sniff the air and bolt, running flat out through the bush.

We told him about the priest who had come asking for him. Joshua looked at us, smiling. "I married my woman in a Catholic church, and that is how my name got in their good book. That was many, many years ago. Maybe I should have asked them to take it off when she died. But it does not matter." I got up and left them to talk as I went about the business of splitting more wood outside.

I had just finished splitting the wood and was piling it when they came out of the cabin. Grandma had a pack-sack over her shoulder and Joshua was carrying her teapot. Grandma said, "Go put the jeans on, Naens. We are going out to clean a moose and bring back some moose meat. We'll wait for you at his place. Run, tell our neighbour to come."

They walked away, talking. A moose. He had killed a moose on the way here last night? I ran first to our neighbour's house. There was that dog again. This time, I paid no attention to him and he quickly lost interest. I made sure I stomped my feet on the platform by the door before I pushed the door open. I never forgot that I was not supposed to knock. They were at the table, just finishing their breakfast. I said, "Grandma says to come get some moose meat. Joshua killed a moose." The man nodded and I turned and left, running all the way home.

By the time I put my jeans on and reached Joshua's cabin, our neighbour was coming along the path behind me. Grandma and Joshua waited for the man, and when he arrived, three more people materialized on the path. In a little over half an hour, there were many people standing around the place waiting, and finally we all followed Joshua up the path toward the railway tracks. I realized that Grandma didn't have to tell me to say anything else to our neighbour. He knew to notify the next person, and that person the next.

When we reached the railroad, there were half a dozen

other people coming along the tracks and they joined the group that trailed out behind us. I nudged Grandma. "Joshua has miraculously grown a very long tail this morning."

I had come to understand that when a moose was killed, everyone was notified as quickly as possible and everyone got a piece of the meat. Since there were no refrigerators or freezers, the moose had to be butchered and eaten quickly.

WINTER AT GRANDMA'S

ONE DAY IN THE FIRST WEEK OF SEPTEMBER, WE SAW a man coming down the hill from the railroad tracks. Normally, our visitors came up the path by the lake. I glanced at Grandma. "How did he find the path from the railroad?"

Grandma raised her eyebrows and we finished tying the new smoke racks we had built around the campfire place. We stopped and waited as the man strolled toward us. He had dark brown curly hair. He was kind of skinny and he wore a navy jacket over a white shirt open at the collar. He was clean shaven and...I was suddenly getting very nervous. I knew who he was.

He came to a stop in front of us. He said, "Hello. My name is Mr. Thompson. I'm your new teacher. You're Ray? The children told me where to find you. And this is your grandmother, Agnes? Hello, how are you?"

I glanced at Grandma. She smiled at him and said in

English, "Hello. Good to meet you. Ray will go to school. She a good girl. She work hard and she learn real fast too."

That was the longest string of English words I had ever heard her utter. I grinned at her and stuck my hand out to shake the teacher's hand. He looked around at the cabin and at the smoke rack. He noted the strips of willow bark we used to tie the racks together. I said, "Better than rope."

He looked at the moosehide Grandma had stretched in the square wooden frame. Suddenly, he burst out with one question after another. He looked like a kid in a candy shop being confronted by hundreds of different kinds of candy. He circled around the rack, pointing to this and that.

Grandma's jaw dropped until I walked by her, brushing her chin up with my finger while the teacher's back was to us. She poked me and I grinned back at her as I attempted to answer the questions fired one after another about the moosehide.

How did one begin, what was to be done next, why? Why this and why that? I asked Grandma, she explained, and I told him. Just as quickly came another question. I asked, she told, I explained. Accustomed as I was to the Ojibwa language now, his English words sounded as if he had a right to know and almost demanded an answer to his questions. Finally, Grandma had had enough and, much to my relief, she went inside the cabin.

I shook my head, and the teacher suddenly stood still

and he shoved his hands into his pockets and looked at me rather sheepishly. I grinned and he started to laugh softly. I said, "That was not a nice thing to do. You had no right to ask so many questions. I don't know if she'll ever talk to you again. But if you would like, I'll let you know when she is ready to do the next stage and you can come and watch – if she says it's okay."

He nodded and pursed his lips. "Better tell her I'm sorry. I promise to behave next time." He swung around and went back up the path.

I stopped at the door and said, "You can come out now, he's gone."

Grandma pulled the door open. She said, "I know he's gone. I did see him walk by. My goodness! One more minute and I would have been mighty tempted to hit him over the head with my walking cane!"

I laughed. "You don't even have a walking cane, Grandma."

She stopped and considered. "Come to think of it, I have wished I had one more often these days. Like when I'm coming down that slope off the railroad tracks or making my way through that mud section at the bottom path. And I would like to have something to bonk that dog on the head when he always runs at me barking his head off." Oh, she was really irritated.

I smiled at her. "Have you seen a branch or a tree that would be just right? I can carve it, you know." I didn't expect the answer she gave me.

"Yes, as a matter of fact, I was looking at a small birch tree that had been bent by a large poplar that had broken off, and it grew right around it. It had formed a perfect handle! Come, let's go get it."

I grabbed the axe and we headed up the hill behind Joshua's place. Joshua had left the next day after the villagers had cleaned up the moose carcass. I couldn't believe how quickly it seemed the whole village showed up at the site – every able-bodied man and woman must have been there. They all had a piece of the moose meat and then they were gone.

I spotted the little tree the minute we entered the clearing. It was perfect. She cut the length of the tree and up to the curved handle. As we came back down the hill, we spotted a partridge on a tree branch. I remembered there was one question I had never got a chance to ask Joshua.

"Grandma, how did Joshua get those partridges when we first arrived at his place? He had two partridges, but he didn't have a gun, a slingshot, or anything. And, I couldn't see him lugging rocks in case he saw a partridge."

She smiled. "What you did not see is that he had a snare wire in his pocket. You should always carry one around when you're out there."

I turned. "Do you have one?"

She shook her head. "Nope, don't need one just now."

I looked up at the partridge again. "It's not a rabbit to be caught in a snare wire, so how does he catch them?"

She continued down the hill. "Well, you get a long, skinny pole and then you attach a snare wire in a loop at the tip. And you very slowly move the snare wire hoop toward the partridge, from the back, and you gradually get the wire around its head, and then you yank down and the wire tightens around its neck and then you have partridge and dumplings for supper." I decided I would like to try that. Maybe when we went out to the bush next time.

Over the next couple of days, I carved the wooden cane with loving care, and when I got to the tip of the handle, there was a well-defined partridge head in the wood. I carved it out and the natural grain of the curve gave it the texture of feathers. Quite pleased with myself, I cut out the eyes and the beak with extra care, then smoothed it out by rubbing it very hard and quick with a piece of rough canvas I found by the woodpile.

I worked alone in the cabin and kept a pot of stew simmering on the stove waiting for Grandma. She had gone again early this morning to see to a very sick person at the other end of the community. This was the third day, and she always came back very tired late in the evening. Then she would work with her herbs and medicine bundles that hung above the ceiling poles.

I had learned never to disturb her, as she hummed and sang under her breath as she worked. I'd just finished rubbing the end tip of the wood when I heard her coming. The ice had formed over the mud puddles and it cracked under her feet. It was getting dark and my neck and back hurt from leaning over the cane all day long. I laid it on her bed. It was white and shiny. A perfect cane, if I might say so myself!

I poured a cup of tea for her and set a bowl of chicken stew at the table as she came in. I noticed right away that she had a smile on her face and she was happy. Then her eyebrows went up as she saw the cane. She walked across and grabbed it, examining it in her hands from one end to the other.

"Wow! This is beautiful. You have a great gift, Naens! There is even the partridge there. The cane was taken from his front yard, after all!" She poked it on the floor and thump-thumped to the table beside me.

I smiled. "Just don't ever poke me on the foot with that thing!"

She giggled and gave me a hug. She sat down to eat with an appetite I had not seen her have in a long time. "Your patient will live?" I asked.

She smiled. "Yes, he'll live. No one thought he would, but there. He sat up and demanded a big meal today. He ate, slept, and when he woke up, he told me to go home. He's still a bit weak, but he was standing outside taking a big breath of fresh air when I left the cabin."

I was getting used to having her gone for long periods of time, tending to sick people. Some came back from the hospital still sick, others refused to go to the hospital altogether. Those were the ones she tended to. There were even times when she was called away to another community. She would get on the train and I would wait at the cabin until she returned.

All too soon, it was a Monday and the first day of school. I got up early and couldn't figure out what to wear. I didn't want to wear my good dresses the first day. What if I was the only one dressed up? In the end, I decided to put one of my new pairs of pants on with my sweater. Grandma tied my hair back into a ponytail. My heart was already pounding when I went across the field to the schoolyard.

I had just reached the path to the school when the teacher came out and shook the bell. Suddenly, kids came running from all directions, and some went in front of me and I could hear others behind me. We all came to a stop in front of the teacher, who yelled for everyone to line up in two rows. Small kids to the left and bigger kids to the right. I stayed in the big kid row where I was. There were taller boys in front of me.

By now, I felt like others must see my heart pounding right through my coat! My knees shook as my line moved to the door after the little ones had gone through. There was a porch area where we took off our shoes. I was glad I had clean socks on, with no holes. I put my boots in the back corner and followed the people into an area where coat hangers hung in rows.

I noticed that the other wall held a low row of hooks where the little ones had hung their coats. I took the far corner hanger and hung up my coat. The older students paid no attention to me, but they greeted each other, with the boys making teasing comments at the girls. I walked behind another girl into the classroom as the teacher directed people where to sit. The girl in front was just as tall as I was. I sat down behind her.

While the rest of the boys were shuffled around, to get the shorter ones to sit in front of the taller ones, the girl turned around and smiled at me. She seemed to examine my face before I asked, "What is your name?"

She smiled and said, "Jane. I know your name is Ray." That was the problem. They all knew me, but I didn't know any of them.

I loved the smell of this room. It smelled of crayons and plasticine. The teacher handed us a page of paper with questions about ourselves, which we filled out while he was with the little ones, and then he gradually made his way up the rows to the bigger students.

That was the beginning of my school year. The students pretty much left me alone. They were friendly and nice, all right, but no one made any attempt to be my friend or to hang around with me.

Friday after school was the Thanksgiving weekend, and Jane and I made our way home. She lived across the railroad tracks and I often walked with her until she took her path off the tracks and I continued down to my turnoff to the path to Grandma's cabin.

Come to think of it, this would be the last time I

walked with her. I usually took the lakeshore path by our neighbour's at lunch and their dog always came to meet me. He didn't bark anymore. He came up wagging his tail, walked with me up to the stand of trees at the edge of his area, and there he stopped.

When we were beyond the train station, I suddenly had an idea. I turned to Jane and asked, "Why don't you come down to the cabin sometime? I'll be there. And we hardly get any visitors."

Jane replied, "Well, you wouldn't, would you? Get visitors, I mean."

I asked, "Why not? What do you mean?"

Jane laughed and smiled at me. "Have you noticed that the other kids don't come and hang around you? How many come and play with you?"

I looked down at my feet poking out left and right beyond my coat as I walked along beside her. I asked, "So, what's wrong with me? What is it they don't like about me?"

Jane laughed out loud. "It's not you, dummy! It's your grandma. People are scared of her!"

I looked at her, quite shocked. "Why would they be scared of her? She's nice to people. She has helped many people here!"

Jane sighed and explained. "They aren't scared because she's bad or anything. They're just scared because she's a very powerful medicine woman. They're afraid that they might do something wrong and make her angry or something."

That was the dumbest thing I had ever heard! I said

nothing more and continued walking. I left her behind me before she stepped off the tracks to her path home. When I got home, Grandma noticed right away and told me to sit down and tell her what was troubling me.

I had never hesitated in telling her the truth when she asked me something, so I told her about the weird conversation. She said nothing at all as I looked at my feet. I had on a brand new pair of moccasins she had made for me after she finished the pair for Joshua. His were to be a Christmas gift for him. I made her wait until Christmas. I was the one who insisted on presents this year, otherwise Joshua and Grandma never did the Christmas gifts stuff.

After awhile, she got up and said, "If your food lay on the other side of a moosehide bridge, would you try not to eat so often, for fear you would wear out the bridge? Or would you cross it often and eat as much as you could, for fear the bridge would rot out from lack of use and repair?"

I smiled. "You know me, I would be a regular glutton." Use it or lose it, as Dave would say.

She was by the stove when she asked, "Well, Glutton, what would you like to have for Thanksgiving dinner?"

Without hesitation, I said, "Trout. Fresh trout, steamed with potatoes, carrots, and onions!"

THANKSGIVING CAME AND WENT and now Christmas was approaching. I was getting all excited and I told Grandma

I was going to decorate our little cabin. She glanced at me but said nothing at all. I cut out paper snowflakes, which I pasted everywhere on the wall. But Grandma wouldn't let me put one on the window, it obstructed her view. Then I went to the store and pulled out the cigarette boxes for the wrappers, just the way we had decorated our tree back home.

One day, I found that Grandma had gone to the store and come home with candies wrapped in red, green, yellow, and blue shiny foil. The foil made perfect stringers! When I had everything pretty much glittering and colourful, the door opened one evening and in came Joshua!

He held out a new pair of snowshoes for Grandma and we burst out laughing. Then he turned around, picked up something else by the door, and held up a new pair of snowshoes for me too! He told us about Fur Ball and how he had begun wandering away from the cabin and, one day, did not return. Joshua had followed his tracks in the snow and, sure enough, way over the hill almost to the railroad tracks, he had found an opening at the base of a rock cliff. That was where Fur Ball's tracks had disappeared. Now that Joshua knew where the cave was, he said he often went by and saw no other tracks around.

Christmas was very quiet at our end of the community. Grandma was really pleased with her tams and Joshua did a little jig in his brand new moccasins. Joshua hung around over the holidays and even got on the train to get some trapping supplies that the storekeeper didn't have. When he returned, he showed up at our cabin with a box. He set it down on the table and indicated that we should open it. I didn't move but waited for Grandma to do the honours. Suddenly, the box moved!

Grandma jumped back, then cautiously approached the box again. She reached out and slowly pulled the flap back, and out popped a white furry thing. It was a little puppy! She turned to Joshua with a strange look on her face. "That was a long time ago. Why?" I stayed where I was, waiting for them to get on with whatever on earth it was they were talking about.

"I told you I would get you another," Joshua said. "I never found one until this morning. There it was! Just like Snow."

Grandma reached in, and out popped a fuzzy white puppy in her hand. Grandma held it up. It was a male, all right. She turned it over and over and sniffed it. I said, "Mama Dog, rest assured that no human scent has contaminated it. You can claim it."

Joshua laughed out loud. That surprised me. In fact, I believe that was the very first time I had ever heard him laugh like that. Grandma came and put the puppy on my lap, saying, "This old man here asked to borrow my beloved dog one day, because he had a big load to haul back to his trapline and it was very late in the spring. My dog was a good sled dog...."

Joshua finished the story. "I slipped and cracked the ice and I quickly sank into the icy water. The dog came to my rescue, but the sled went through the thin ice and it pulled the dog down with it. I couldn't reach him."

I picked up the dog and said, "So here he is. What did you call him? Snow? Looks more like a Snow Ball to me."

His hair was thick and bushy and his two little black button eyes poked out from the thick white fur around his face. "Well, bring Snow Ball over here and see if he wants some milk," Grandma said. I took the puppy to her and poured a cup of tea for Joshua. Next, I emptied a cardboard box, which I lined with some chinking batten we had left over from the cabin patch-up in the fall.

The puppy whimpered and Grandma rushed outside with it. Ah, that too. I forgot about that. I told Joshua about Dave and the baby moose that had peed all over the floor back home. That story caught him just as he had taken a big sip of tea, and his quick laughter sent a spray of tea all over his knees! Grandma had a giggling fit while I found a towel to throw at Joshua to wipe up with.

January began another round of school, week after week, into February and March. The teacher came several times to inquire if Grandma was working on any leather or anything. But Grandma suddenly had to go somewhere whenever she saw him coming. She said he was very ill mannered and showed no respect, and that she had no patience for his endless questions!

I smiled. Yes, to Grandma, he was totally opposite to

what he should be. The very way he was taught to learn, and the way he taught, was opposite to the way I was learning from Grandma. I didn't blurt out questions about things I should figure out for myself with Grandma. Yet that was what this teacher expected me to do in school. With Grandma, I was to understand something, and with the teacher, I needed only to memorize something. And he, being a stranger, should never have asked her any questions at all, unless she had invited him to do so. Needless to say, she did not like him at all! I, on the other hand, soaked up all the knowledge I could get from him.

I spent many hours with the teacher doing extra work, since I was working at several grades above the rest of the students in class. They didn't have high school in this community, so I had to do extra work beyond the textbooks the rest worked from. Although there were many students older than I, it was clear that their first language was Ojibwa and they were having difficulties making the switch to the foreign English way of thinking and speaking.

For this reason, the teacher took great comfort in finding a student who could learn just as quickly as he taught a new concept. I had the curiosity and the enthusiasm of someone who longed to see the rest of the world as well as the land around me. I loved the stories of faraway places, as well as the mysteries under my feet when I walked through the swamp with Grandma.

I learned much during those winter months.

Springtime came quickly with warm, wet, and dripping days that turned the paths into ice in the cold nights. Grandma was full of energy and spent her days teaching the dog new tricks and obedience to her motion commands. Snow Ball was trained not to rush out to meet me, but stayed by the door; if it was a stranger, he would bark several times but remain where he was until Grandma came out.

Grandma was very strict that Snow Ball was going to be a responsible working dog and that he must not run around like crazy and bark his head off for no apparent reason. We still played though. Snow Ball and I had snow ball fights. I would throw snow balls at him and he'd try to catch them. Soon, he was able to grab every ball I threw. Even Grandma laughed from the doorway when he jumped up very high to snap the snow ball in his mouth. Oh, he was so proud of himself when he did.

He was now the size of most of the full-grown dogs, but just a little clumsy puppy yet. He had taken to helping me pull the toboggan load of dry wood, and he didn't complain anymore when Grandma put his leather collar on and laced him to his dogsled. At every down-slope, he learned to wait for me to catch up and grab the end rope to hold the toboggan back before he'd go downhill. Otherwise, the toboggan would overtake him as he went down.

I spent a lot of time with Snow, checking rabbit snares

and hauling wood, getting water, and doing chores around the cabin when Grandma wasn't home. I hadn't realized how busy she was.

THE SNOW DISAPPEARED and the yellow grass was soon covered with new green grass. I had noticed Grandma was very quiet these days. Most times she went off alone with Snow Ball when I had to do my homework. I went to get some water once, and when I returned, I saw her sitting on her bed looking at her hands. I sat down on the bench at the table and said, "I have seen you twice now, sitting like that looking at your hands. What is it that you're thinking?"

She looked at me with a soft smile on her face and heaved a big sigh. "I'm just thinking and talking to my hands in my mind."

I sat there waiting and she continued. "I asked my hands what they did this winter. How did I make this world a better place for someone? I remember how my hands looked when I was a child, then when I was a young woman, when I had my children, and on and on through the years of my life. I remember and cherish the memories. I thank the Creator for all that and then I think of the days to come, and of you."

I smiled and said, "'Taking stock of your life,' I think is what the teacher would say."

She stood up, "I won't even think about anything that remotely sounds like 'smacking dirty socks on my life!'"

I sat there grinning. "Not 'stockings,' Grandma."

She pulled her boots on at the door and went out. She really didn't like me talking about the teacher, I thought. I was learning so much from him that I often came home bursting with new information that I would tell Grandma about, but she always seemed irritated afterward. Maybe she thought all the new information would make me forget the things she was teaching me. I needed to show her I would not forget.

I picked up my half-finished carving of Snow Ball. I sat whittling for a long time until I finished the tail. It was Snow Ball sitting on a pile of snow. I was thinking of Fur Ball when my hand became still. I went outside to where Grandma was seated by the campfire, making a pot of tea. I sat down beside her and asked, "Grandma, when Joshua brought Snow Ball, do you think that he did it so we could never see Fur Ball again?"

She stopped and thought awhile before she said, "Snow Ball must never meet Fur Ball. We can't go any-where without Snow Ball. It would definitely be in Fur Ball's best interests that he does not get comfortable being around other people. You have a point there, but you know? Joshua does not think like that. If he didn't want us ever to see Fur Ball again, he would have told us. I think that when he first saw Snow Ball, he truly knew that Snow Ball belonged to us."

I hesitated before I could bring myself to admit what was also bothering me. "Summer is almost here, Grandma, and then I will have to go back to Mama in the fall. How will you manage with Snow Ball if you have to go away to look after sick people?"

She turned to look at me and then she smiled. "Ha, maybe that is why he brought Snow Ball to us! Just to make sure you stay here with me for a long time!"

I smiled then. Not to worry. Grandma said so.

GRANDMA BEGAN ASKING ME to accompany her in her travels over the hills and swamps beyond Joshua's cabin. She carried a birchbark basket with the handle draped over her arm as she collected her spring medicinal plants. Each plant she released from the soil was replaced with a pinch of tobacco.

"Always leave a 'thank you' for everything you take from the soil, or it will be like you have taken it without its permission and it will be no good to you," she said.

She pointed out many plants as we walked along, stopping to pick some; others she left until they matured more. She explained the uses and preparation for each. It was difficult, but I memorized which plants were used for this and that and which plant had poisonous roots but medicinal leaves, or the other way around.

There were some that you could only scrape the bark from and the rest was poisonous. Some plants looked almost the same, but one was medicinal and the other was poisonous. Even then, there were exceptions to the poisonous plants, depending on time and preparation method. I decided to leave that until later. It was much too confusing otherwise.

I awoke very early one morning and realized my time had come. Everything was very quiet. Grandma had explained to me what to expect and what to do. I had some pads made up ready for use when the time came. I looked at the bag hanging on the bed beside me as I lay there. I felt nothing strange in my body. Perhaps if I rolled off the bed, I wouldn't get any blood on my bedding. I reached for the bag and rolled off the bed and went down on my knees on the floor, right on top of Snow Ball's tail! The dog yelped in pain, I screamed, and Grandma jumped up on her elbow, demanding, "What? What's the matter?"

I sat there on the floor and I felt laughter bubbling up inside me. Snow Ball was standing there, tail wagging, and looking kind of sheepish. I laughed silently as I got to my feet, "I am all bloody, but I saved my blanket."

Grandma did not move as I slipped on my shoes and went outside. I washed and cleaned myself beside the cabin where our wash water barrel stood. It was very damp and a bit cool. Today was exactly one month before my fourteenth birthday. Grandma had said that on this day would be the end of my childhood. I was a young woman now. And I had so much yet to learn. I was scared.

I came in and Grandma was already up, fussing around at the table. I went past her without a word and began fixing up my bedding. "What was Snow Ball doing inside the cabin? I didn't even hear you let him in last night," I said as I tried to go about my daily routine.

Grandma laughed as she set a pan of bacon on the stove. "I sneaked ever so quietly out of the cabin to go to the outhouse last night and I didn't close the door all the way. I didn't bother taking the flashlight either. When I came back in, I was near my bed when a cold wet nose nudged my hand. Near gave me a heart attack, that dog."

I knew I had to wait until my period was over before I would be allowed to accompany Grandma again on her wanderings over the hills and swamps. I stayed home and did my homework again that day. I smiled as I remembered the time I'd had an idea that would greatly help my job of memorizing the plants. I had drawn a sketch of a plant that was particularly medicinally strong but equally poisonous. Grandma saw the sketch and, very slowly and deliberately, she tore the page and put it into the stove.

"Shhh. Keep the plant inside you only. It does not belong on a page of paper."

I smiled. I had suddenly understood that knowledge of this sort did not belong in the culture of "paper." Nothing was ever said about that again. Nothing was said of Joshua either.

We each knew that we were waiting and that now it was almost time to begin worrying. He should have been here as soon as the ice went out, but there was still no sign of him. Grandma would know if and when it was time to do something.

Late one night, I awoke to the sound of Grandma rummaging around in the dark inside a box at the corner of the table. "What are you doing, Grandma?"

Her voice came back, "Looking for a candle. I had a dream about that old man. I dreamt he was standing on an island surrounded by fog and he kept gesturing to me and I...didn't know what he was trying to say to me. Old Fool!"

I was up on my elbow when she struck a match and lit a candle. "Now, you can't get mad at him because you dreamt about him. You know what he'd say? 'Agnes, Old Woman, if you had just told me how much you cared for me....'" I didn't even see her old moccasin coming, that hit me right on the face.

THE SEAGULL
SUMMER 1982

SCHOOL WAS ALMOST OVER AND I WAS TRYING TO finish the last assignment. The teacher would be gone in a couple of weeks. Grandma had gone off with Snow Ball in the canoe to check the fishnet and I was still here tapping my pencil on the paper. It was the last writing exercise and I had not a clue what to write about! I got up and went outside.

As soon as I closed the door, I caught the whiff of birch-bark smoke. Since it wasn't from our stove, I rushed down the path and, sure enough, there was smoke coming out of Joshua's stovepipe! I ran up the path to his cabin, but just as I got to the door, I heard a board fall on the ground behind the cabin. I ran around the corner and stopped. A huge black bear whirled around from the woodpile and our eyes locked! My heart pounded so hard against my throat that I could not move. The bear snorted and swung his head back and forth and took one step toward me, then another.

I stood there and it stopped. I saw its nostrils twitch side to side and my mind went to the door. I could run in there. I turned, and no sooner had I moved when I felt the impact on my side. I fell in a rolling motion and sprawled with my face to the ground! The bear was right on top of me and I could feel its breath on the back of my neck! A paw came down and swiped up under my arm, and it flipped me right over onto my back! Then I was face to face with the bear and...it began licking my face with some excitement.

My hands landed on each side of his face and I pushed his head back at arm's length. "Fur Ball? Is that you, Fur Ball?"

Suddenly, Joshua's voice rang out in Ojibwa. "Let her go! Come here! What are you doing here, anyway, Fur Ball?" He sounded very irritated.

Fur Ball turned around and walked to Joshua and lay down in front of him. Joshua put his hands on his hips and sighed, looking at me. "Are you all right?"

I had jumped up as soon as Fur Ball was off of me and now I stood uncertain as to what to do. "I'm okay."

My glance indicated the bear with a question and Joshua said, "Come inside. I thought I had sneaked away on him. But, as you can see, he tracked me here. I did manage to go to the store for the supplies, though. I just got back. He must have just got here, because he wasn't around when I came in. I saw that Agnes's canoe was gone, so I thought there was no one home when I walked by."

I noticed the boxes then, two of them stacked by the door. With sudden anxiety, I jumped up. "Grandma will be back soon, very soon. She's got Snow Ball with her. Fur Ball, can you tie him up? What if he wanders over there? No, Snow Ball will follow my scent; he'll find me!"

Joshua smiled. "Shhh. Don't get excited. Tell me how the winter went." I spoke fast and kept glancing out the window that faced the path. Finally, he seemed satisfied that I'd told him all he needed to know. Then he said, "I will have to go right now. I left the canoe by the rock cliff along the railroad tracks. I didn't feel like carrying the canoe over and over the portages and lugging the boxes over."

He smiled as he looked at me. His eyes looked creamy, not as white and alert as I remembered them. He seemed very tired. "Are you all right, Joshua? Do you feel well?"

He smiled. "I am all right. I'm just getting too old for my way of life, I think. It is a lot of work out there. For the first time this winter, I longed for hours by the stove, listening to other people around me...."

I said, softly, "We would have come, but we have Snow Ball...."

Joshua finished, "and I have Fur Ball. He showed up first thing in the spring, looking for food. Luckily, I had just pulled up my fishnet. He didn't even wait until they were cooked. Now, I just throw him a fish and he'll eat it right there."

I added, "Now that he has followed you here, this is where he will come if he should notice you gone again."

He looked at me. "How does Agnes do it?"

I raised my eyebrows and he explained. "How does Agnes keep up with you? I had not even reached there yet, and here you already said it." I felt chastised. I put my head down. That was his to say and I should have waited for him to speak it. Those were his words to speak and not mine!

He stood up and grabbed his packsacks. I forced myself to sit quietly and wait until it was time for my next move or to say something else. I watched him empty the boxes and pack the things into the sacks. I remained still, pushing the thought of the dog and the bear far back in my mind. I would wait in case he thought of something to say.

"Oh, I nearly forgot. Tell Agnes she found that plant she was searching for. If you both and Snow Ball can come to the last portage from my cabin sometime this summer, she can paddle over and I will tell her all about it."

I smiled. "We'll do that." He stopped and looked at me; then, shaking his head, he stooped to pick up one of the packsacks, chuckling under his breath. He had looked at me and thought what he saw was funny? I picked up the other sack and we went out.

He went back in, fussing around inside the cabin, putting the fire out and locking the door, while I stood perfectly still, allowing Fur Ball to sniff and examine every part of my body. I refrained from touching him or making any welcoming gesture to him. Soon, he had satisfied himself that I was indeed the human being he used to know, but showed no interest or sign of recognition, so he turned with a huff and trotted off toward Joshua without a backward glance.

Joshua had hoisted up his load on his back and was ready to go when I went to him, pulling off my scarf from around my hair. "Would it be a good idea to put this around his neck when there's a chance of seeing people, so they'll know he's with you?"

He stopped, looking at Fur Ball for a second before he smiled. "Yes, I think that would be a good idea." He reached for the scarf and went to put it around Fur Ball's neck and I saw the bear's eyes widen. Joshua glanced at me.

"Your scent must be strong on the scarf."

Of course! I hadn't thought of that. Soon it would disappear though. Especially on him! Oh, he stank of bear musk and sweat. I smiled and watched them walk away, and soon they disappeared among the bushes and then there was no sound.

I turned and walked back to our cabin. What did he mean, "She found that plant she was searching for?" Didn't Grandma know all the plants? Wouldn't she know if she had found what she was searching for? I didn't get it. Maybe it was one plant that could also be used in place of another plant at another time of year. Grandma would tell me.

I went in and began writing about Joshua and Fur Ball and their visit to the community. I had just finished the last sentence when the door opened and Grandma came in. "Are you finished? Go fetch the fish for me. I got three big, beautiful trout!"

I smiled. "Yes, I am done. Joshua was just here, but he had to leave right away because Fur Ball showed up at his door when he had just returned from the store." Grandma stopped, looked at the floor for a few seconds, but did not say anything. She looked very disappointed.

I got up and ran to the door and down the path. When I returned with the fish, she was preparing to get the fire going outside at the campfire. I told her about Joshua and Fur Ball and all that he had said. She was very pleased that he was well, but did not like the fact that the bear had tracked him to his cabin in the community.

AS SOON AS SCHOOL WAS OVER, we headed out to our usual campsite. Grandma had laughed when I pulled my camp clothes out of the box from under the bed. I had really grown, so I had to throw aside some of my shirts, but the sweaters were fine. The stretchy pants were just that – stretchy enough for me to get into again this year.

By early afternoon, we were paddling along the shoreline, heading for one of the last islands on the lake. That was the seagull breeding area, and already they were flying around and around above us. As we passed by one of the

rocky reefs that was just deafening with squawking seagulls, I saw a fuzzy little thing floating on the waves in
front of the canoe.

As we approached, the baby seagull turned its head,
but made no move to get out of the way. All it did was
tuck its head down over its shoulders, trying to look like
just a little floating fuzz ball. Grandma spoke softly
behind me. "It is probably an outcast. Probably lost its
mama or its mama lost it, or the mama died somewhere.
Anyway, that, there, is an orphaned seagull, run off the
rocky reef by the adults."

I had stopped paddling and now I put my paddle in
and held it there, stopping the forward motion of the
canoe. Grandma put her paddle across her lap, and I
knew she was waiting for me to think of the pros and
cons of picking up the seagull. If I did not pick him up,
he would starve to death by late tomorrow afternoon or
earlier. He already looked like he had been through an
awful time. If I picked him up, I could raise him and
bring him back in the fall and let him join the others for
the trip back south. I had to.

I reached out and slowly put my hand under his little
feet and lifted him out of the water. His head popped out
when he realized he was floating in space on top of a
giant's hand. I could feel the fluttering of his tiny heart
against my fingers. A towel landed beside me and I lowered the baby seagull into the towel.

I smiled at Grandma. "He's just a little fuzz ball. Look

at the little spikes on his head."

Grandma smiled. "Wait until a few minutes after you feed him, he will start pooping all over the place and he'll always be looking for food to eat."

I smiled back, saying, "I guess we'll just have to keep feeding him until he's big and strong. Then he'll have to learn to fend for himself." Grandma continued to paddle on behind me by herself.

Grandma said no more until we reached shore at the little island where we usually camped. I got off and put the baby seagull, still wrapped in the towel, under a shady bush. He made no effort to try to escape. He lay, nodding off, head drooping, then lifting for a second before it drooped forward again.

Snow Ball jumped out and went to examine the towel, but its contents held no interest for him at all. He ran off to check out the campsite. I held the canoe for Grandma to get out, and we pulled the canoe up and proceeded to set up camp. We lugged our food box along with my box of clothes. I dumped my clothes on the ground, pulled some moss to line the cardboard box, and gently lowered the baby seagull into it. He seemed in a panic for a minute, until I started shoving in branches and more moss and finally he settled down again.

I left the box there under a little patch of cedar trees. We set up camp quite quickly now, each doing our usual tasks. Then I went in search of my usual stack of pine branches for the floor of our tent.

I had gotten very good at this and, very quickly, I had five good bundles ready for laying out inside the tent. Snow Ball hadn't stayed with me very long in the bush. There he lay, stretched out in the shade beside the box. I checked the little critter and his head was still bent over his right wing. He was breathing very fast but still sitting upright. I figured that was a good sign. He was just taking a well deserved rest.

Grandma was nowhere around when I emerged from the tent. I guessed she was off doing her thing, because the canoe was not where we had pulled in. She always went to the mainland to set some rabbit snares. Sure enough, I heard the steady drip of the paddle as she came around the island. I had already got a fire going, and she came up giggling. I wanted to know what was so funny, and there she was holding up a big jackfish!

"Right at the shore, I had given up and was just pulling up the line when it hit! Oh, my! Did it ever fight. I was hoping you would come down and see me pull it up right onto the land!"

I too giggled. I loved my Grandma so dearly, right at that moment. I had discovered that her white teeth, which she always indicated as proof of why one should not eat candies, turned out to be false teeth. She wore her dentures most of the time, but some days, she didn't bother putting them in, like when we went camping. So now, when she laughed out loud, you only saw the toothless void of her mouth.

Her thick scarf was pulled low over her forehead, her thick black sweater buttoned at the neck, and her thick blue-flowered cotton dress hung straight over her beige cotton-stocking-covered legs. On her feet were two black ladies' running shoes with a pair of white socks pulled up over her ankles. Those were her comfy, camping, old-Indian-lady clothes, she had once said when I suggested she should try on a pair of stretch slacks.

She had worn her tams alternately whenever she went to the store. They were her "dress-up" hats. And only on those occasions did she put her teeth in too.

Grandma had just finished cleaning the fish and I had the frying pan ready over the fire, when we heard the squawk from the box and saw it shake as the baby seagull decided to come to life.

"The Fuzz Ball is hungry," I said.

Grandma laughed. "Fuzz Ball is not an appropriate name for that thing in the box. In a couple of weeks, he will turn into something very drastically different. Maybe he will have turned into a monster of some kind by then."

I smiled. Perhaps. Fuzz Ball squawked again as I approached. In this short time, I had already noticed that the little guy squawked every time I walked near his box.

When we finished eating, I broke the fish into soft pieces and fed Fuzz Ball. He seemed to have trouble swallowing the dry flesh, so I added some liquid and dripped the pieces into his open mouth. Now he gulped them down one after the other.

In the days after that, he greedily gobbled up the little minnows I caught in my mosquito netting. Then he swallowed the baby fish I caught in my miniature fishnet that I threw off shore. After that, he was big enough to march around our campsite and kick pots aside if they contained no food for him.

He also took to rummaging around in Grandma's medicine bag. That one got him into trouble. Grandma shoved her hand into the bottom of her bag and grabbed his beak when he went to check what she had for him. However, that didn't do any good. So Grandma crammed the bag's contents into a five-pound lard pail. She clamped down the lid and there was no way even a seagull could get into it.

As the days and weeks went by, we went back to Grandma's cabin several times to replenish supplies, sell our blueberries, and call Mama. On our last trip there, we were finally able to relax and enjoy the summer when we got the answer from Mama that she would let me stay with Grandma forever.

We also found out that she was expecting a baby. When it was time for its birth around Christmastime, Grandma and I would travel to visit them. I didn't know how I felt about that news until I thought about Cindy. Then I knew that a baby brother or sister would be just what Cindy needed right now. As for me, I would have a half-brother or sister — a half of Mama and half of Dave.

At that moment, the seagull hopped up to my lap and

pulled on my lower lip. The silly thing thought he was half a seagull and the other half human! That was the sum experience of his life, which was more than most seagulls could say, I suppose.

Toward the end of July, we decided to camp on the island first before we set off to visit Joshua. The next morning, I awoke to hear something rustling against the tent wall. Grandma was still in her bedding. We had slept in, because a thunderstorm had kept us awake most of the night.

We both got out of bed and Grandma flung the tent door-flap open and there was Fuzz Ball, hopping around on top of Grandma's crumpled jacket on the ground, and we burst out laughing.

He whirled around and there he stood facing us, with Grandma's upper dentures clamped in his beak! All I saw was big teeth and skinny legs! We just sat there rocking in hysterical laughter, until Grandma dove to grab him when he decided to run away from the noise we were making.

She tackled him to the ground and retrieved her teeth, and Fuzz Ball dove to safety between Snow Ball's legs. He had apparently decided to check her pockets as he always did, looking for treats. Grandma had taken to carrying wrapped candies in her pocket to lure him in and out of the canoe or wherever she wanted him to go.

The other pocket almost always contained her false teeth, which she would slip into her mouth whenever she needed to chew something. That morning the seagull became known as False Teeth the Seagull.

We headed out that morning to Joshua's cabin. As we crossed the lake, False Teeth still rode on top of Grandma's lap. The rocking motion of her body didn't seem to affect him as he lay snuggled inside her buttoned sweater. Although he could fly, there was no way he would leave us while we travelled. Sometimes, he would hop down and wander up and down over the boxes and bags inside the canoe, as he was doing now, if he wasn't pestering Snow Ball, who was curled up in the bottom of the canoe at Grandma's feet.

We heard the airplane coming long before we saw it. As the pilot spotted us, the plane swerved down, tipping its wing as I waved. That was when False Teeth screeched and dove for safety right under Grandma's armpit, and would not come out, even after the plane was gone! Now I called him False Teeth the Chicken Seagull.

At the first portage, False Teeth hung around waiting to see if we were going to settle down and cook something for him to eat, but when he noticed that we had no intention of doing so, he flew off. We portaged over to the next lake and over to the next beyond that without a sign of him.

When we finally reached the site where Grandma had killed the bear, I knew we had only one more portage to go through. At the last portage, there was a small campsite at a point of land beside the portage trail, and that is where Grandma decided we would set up camp.

The mosquitoes were just as bad as we remembered them. I even rubbed some mosquito repellent on Snow Ball's ears and around his face. We set up the mosquito netting inside the tent and had just settled down to have a quiet meal by the fire when False Teeth showed up. He landed beside Snow Ball, marched to his spot beside Grandma, and nudged her hand for his food.

Without glancing at him, Grandma continued talking to me as she fed him. I said nothing as I listened, and slowly I began to understand to the fullest extent what my mother had agreed to. I swallowed and remained still as Grandma's soft voice continued like wind blowing in from the darkness that now surrounded us.

I had been learning from Grandma about the things she did, but up until this moment, I had not realized she was training me to walk with her in her work and learn of her knowledge, so that I might one day take that which her hands held when hers were no more.

I glanced down at my hands. I had wondered what she meant, when she said that she knew what her hands looked like as a child, as a grown woman, as a...? I knew! Now, I understood! As the years passed, if I wanted to do this, I would watch my hands grow older and remember.... I looked at Grandma and there was a twinkle in her eye. I smiled back. Each wrapped in our own thoughts, we went to bed in silence.

When I awoke the next morning, I was alone. Here I would remain to think on what she had said, until such time as she thought I was ready. Snow Ball was outside by the fire when I came out. I thought that I would have much preferred to be on an island away from the mosquitoes. And I also did not like the thought of camping on the main shoreline.

A bear could come. It might smell my cooking and it would kill Snow Ball, because I knew he would try to protect me. I had just fetched a pail of water when False Teeth came circling above me. I knew it was him. Grandma had put a blueberry stain on the tip of his left wing to mark him and periodically restained it when it started to wear off.

Now he came down and landed right beside the fire. How on earth did he know when I was about to make breakfast? "Did you see Grandma?" I asked. He squawked. "Did she get there all right?" He squawked again.

Grandma had trained him to respond. Too bad he couldn't understand me, or perhaps too bad I couldn't understand him.

After we had a breakfast of leftover food from yesterday's supper, I decided to go set some snares. Snow Ball walked with me as we made our way along the swampy, muddy shoreline. Soon we came upon a cedar stand with many rabbit droppings in piles. They looked like little green peas. Fresh. I knelt and set several snares. I thought about things as I walked.

Did becoming a medicine woman mean people would be afraid of me too? That I would never get married and have children? No, of course Grandma had been married. I smiled as I crawled over a fallen log. I wouldn't be here if she had not. But who was going to marry me if no one was even willing to come visit me? Time would bring what it needed to make things happen. I was not going to be worried about that.

What about school? I realized there was no need to stop going to school. I could learn from the teacher and learn from Grandma at the same time. Yes, I would do what Grandma said and I would learn as fast as I could and never forget things. Snow Ball and I raced back to the campsite and he stayed right beside me all the way.

When I came around the corner of the tent, there was Grandma arriving in the canoe! I ran down to the shore and pulled the canoe up. She said nothing and did not move either. I stayed there, holding the canoe, and waited.

Finally, she lifted her head and spoke. "He must have just gone to sleep and never woke up. His boots are by the door. His blankets are pulled over him. Very recently. About three days ago, I would say." A shock went over me, but there were no words I could think of to say.

I pulled the canoe further up and helped her out to dry land. Snow Ball was there waiting and he licked her hands all over, as if she had been gone a long time. It was too late to head back to the community, so we decided to stay the night and leave early the next morning and let the people look after Joshua's body.

That evening as we sat around the fire, I remembered what Joshua had said. "Grandma, I guess you will never know now. Joshua said he was going to tell you about it when you came." Her eyes glistened in the flickering flame, waiting.

I continued. "He told me to tell you that you had already found that plant you were looking for."

She smiled and barely above a whisper, I heard her say, "I know what he was going to say to me. The plant I had been searching for is you."

I looked at her closely, but I only saw the shadows playing over her face from the flickering campfire. So Joshua had decided I would be the best person for Grandma to train? Why had he looked at me with such an amused glance the last time I saw him?

I nudged at Grandma's foot and said, "Just before he turned to go out, that last time I saw him at his cabin, he looked at me and laughed to himself as he went out the door. What do you think he was thinking? What a fine medicine woman I would make with my green eyes and brown face?"

Grandma's voice shook as she softly whispered, "Would you want to mess with a very strong, young, green-eyed medicine woman?" I said nothing and she added, "You are someone who can handle both worlds – the Native and the non-Native, the old and the new. Someone who can learn the knowledge of the past and carry it forward into the future. That was what Joshua was talking about as the time past and the time yet to come...." Her words trailed away and she seemed lost in thought.

Tears filled my eyes and I let them silently flow over my cheeks as I watched Grandma wiping her face as she headed for the tent. I sat awhile by the fire. "You knew, right at the beginning, didn't you, Joshua?"

ABOUT THE AUTHOR

RUBY SLIPPERJACK has three novels to her credit – *Weesquachak and the Lost Ones*, *Silent Words*, and *Honour the Sun*. She is an assistant professor in the Department of Indigenous Learning at Lakehead University in Thunder Bay, Ontario, and received the William A. West Education Medal for being the highest-ranking Masters of Education graduate at Lakehead University. She is also an accomplished visual artist and a certified First Nations hunter.

An Ojibwa, Ruby Slipperjack was born on her father's trapline at Whitewater Lake, Ontario, and has lived in Winnipeg, Manitoba, and Prince Albert, Saskatchewan, as well as her long-time home of Thunder Bay.